MW00875988

MOVIN' DIFFERENT 3

A HOOD MILLIONAIRE ROMANCE

KEVINA HOPKINS

Movin' Different 3: A Hood Millionaire Romance

Copyright © 2022 by Kevina Hopkins

All rights reserved.

Published in the United States of America.

Published by Cole Hart Signature, LLC.

Mailing List

To stay up to date on new releases, plus get information on contests, sneak peeks, and more,

Go To The Website Below...

www.colehartsignature.com

PREVIOUSLY ON MOVIN'
DIFFERENT 2...

I wiped my palms on the front of my pants before calling McKenzie via FaceTime. Talking to her wasn't enough. I wanted to see her face as well.

I was nervous as hell about calling her. What if she hated me and didn't answer? What if she was laid up with some nigga right now? All of those thoughts left my mind when her beautiful face popped up on the screen.

"Helllooo, Malakai, are you going to say something?" she sang into the phone with her angelic voice. I smiled hearing her say my name because she refused to call me Blaze. She and my mother were the only people that called me Malakai to this day.

"Hey, McKenzie, I'm here. How are you and the kids doing?"

"We're doing good, they're getting so big now," McKenzie said as she flipped the camera on her phone and showed me the twins. They were both sitting up in their play pen playing with toys. She had sent me pictures of them a couple months ago, but they were way bigger now.

"I can't wait until I can see them in person again. I ordered some things for them, and it should be there in couple days," I told her. Even though I wasn't with McKenzie anymore, I still made sure to send stuff for both her and the kids. She told me that I didn't have to, but I wanted to. I owed her that much because I promised I would be there for them no matter what. That's why they were added to my will. If anything ever happened to me, they would be getting something the same way Tasia, Tamika, and my kids would.

"Thank you, how are you doing though?"

"I'm good, ma, I just really needed to hear your voice. I miss you so fucking much, Kenzie. I hope you can bring yourself to forgive me when all of this is over," I said.

"Is everything alright, Malakai?"

Ouch, she didn't tell me that she missed me. I hate to admit it, but that hurt.

"Everything's fine, I just needed to hear your beautiful voice and let you know I missed you. I regret ending things with us, but I still think it was the best thing to do to keep you safe. All of this will be over soon, and I'll spend the rest of my life making this up to you. I still love you just as much as I did when I left."

McKenzie got me sitting here feeling like a bitch right now. I'd never had a problem with confessing my feelings. It's the rejection part I had a problem with, but I needed to let her know all of this while I had a chance.

McKenzie was silent for a minute and put me on pause. I thought she was about to hang up until I heard her sniffling. She was tugging on a nigga's heart strings right now. She had me ready to say fuck this mission but if I did that, then this would all be for nothing.

"I'm sorry, McKenzie, I didn't mean to make you cry. I

understand if you don't feel the same way. You don't even have to say it back. I just needed a reason to smile for a minute. I have some business I need to go take care of, so I'll talk to you later." I was about to hang up until McKenzie unpaused the screen.

"Malakai... I love you too," she said before hanging up the phone. All it took was seeing her face and I felt a hundred times better. I got up from the bed and took a quick shower. I was ready now more than ever to get this over with since I knew it was a chance it would be a happy reunion between Kenzie and me.

The guys and I went over the plan one more time, then we were out of the house and headed to Elijah's warehouse. We were going to murk everyone in there and take their supply. We were rolling in twenty deep. We got dropped off a block away and headed to the warehouse on foot. We had ten minutes to take care of everyone, then our drivers would come to the front to pick us up and the products.

We all put our ski masks on our faces and ran up in the warehouse. Guns were blazing everywhere. It was like a scene from a gangster movie. Some of our men were getting hit and so were theirs. That was the casualty of war. I made my way to the back where I knew Elijah's office was. I kicked in the door, and the fat motherfucker was so engrossed in Kim sucking his dick that he didn't see me coming.

"That's enough, baby, I'll take it from here. Unless you want that fat nigga's cum in your mouth, then I'll wait." I shrugged.

"Thank God, the shit couldn't even stay hard. You owe me double for this shit," she replied.

"Don't worry, you'll be compensated well," I told her.

"Alright, I guess I'll leave you gentlemen to it then," she stated before walking out.

"Come on, son, we can work something out. You don't have to do this. I have kids and grandkids."

"Fuck your kids and grandkids. You didn't think about my family when you had niggas running up in my baby mama's crib," I bellowed.

"I was never going to hurt any of them. I did it to send a warning," he stuttered.

"Well, here's my response to your warning, fat mother-fucker." I lifted my nine and sent a bullet to his head. I let another one off for good measure before walking out of the office.

I went to find my other men, and there were bodies all over the place. My men that weren't injured were helping the injured ones up and taking them out of the building. The rest of them were loading the product and money into a truck. We had hit the motherfucking jackpot and all this shit was over. I could finally go back to Chicago and build the life I wanted with McKenzie. Unfortunately, that thought was short lived when I felt bullets riddling my body. I'm guessing one of Elijah's men must have been hiding somewhere while everything was going down.

I could hear my brother yelling my name and someone returning fire as my body hit the ground. My life flashed before my eyes, and the last picture in the frame of my thoughts was McKenzie's smiling face. If I had to die, at least I could die a happy man knowing the woman I'm in love with loves me too.

CHAPTER ONE

MARTEZ

Today had been a long day, now Lauren and I finally had some alone time and I was enjoying every minute of it. I was taking my time making sweet love to my fiancée. I was deep stroking the pussy, making sure she felt all nine inches of this dick.

Lately, we'd both been busy and barely had time to spend with each other. I'd been busy with the warehouse and starting a new business. Lauren, on the other hand, had been working her ass off to plan our wedding. We had about three months left and she wanted everything to be perfect.

I offered to pay for a wedding planner, but Lauren said it was a waste of money. She said our family was capable of doing everything, so I dropped the subject and allowed her to do her. If she needed my input or opinion, I gave it but other than that, I had no clue of what was going on. The ball was in her court and I allowed her to do her.

I aimed to keep Lauren happy, and she had been patient with me, so I was willing to do whatever she needed. I was fine with having a small wedding or hell, even going to the courthouse, but that was out of the question. Our family was more excited about our big day than we were. When they found out I proposed last year, they couldn't wait to help Lauren start planning.

"Oh my god, Tez, right there, baby, please don't stop. I'm about to cummm," Lauren moaned in my ear. We had been in a heated session for almost an hour and I was on the verge of nutting with her.

"You ready to have my son? I think Kenna need a brother. I'm about to nut in this pussy," I grunted as I hit her spot.

"Noooo," she cried out breathlessly.

I chuckled and pulled out, making sure to bust on her stomach and not in her.

"Get up, cry baby, so we can take a shower," I told her.

Lauren and I climbed out of bed and went inside the bathroom. I got the water started while she brushed her hair into a ponytail. We took a quick shower then climbed into bed together.

"Were you really going to nut in me?" Lauren asked as she laid her head on my chest.

"No, baby, I wouldn't do that to you. We agreed to wait until after the wedding. I know you need to be able to fit your dress, but just know I ain't wasting no time busting in you after we say I do."

"You won't have to wait. I want to try for a boy too. It's just my dress is expensive as hell and we both agreed that when we have our second child we'll officially be married."

I was about to respond when Lauren's phone started to ring. It was after midnight and she normally didn't get calls this late, so I already knew something was going on. I leaned over on the nightstand and picked up her phone. I looked at the screen and saw that it was Mason.

"Here, it's Mason," I told her as I handed her the phone.

"Hey cousin, Tez is right here with me and you're on speaker phone," Lauren said into the phone.

"Hey y'all, how are you two doing?"

"We're good, how are you?"

"I'm hanging in there. I was calling because some shit went down tonight, and Blaze was shot."

"Oh my god, is he okay?" Lauren asked as she sat up in bed.

"Rafael and our team of doctors are working on him right now. He was shot six times, three bullets hit his vest and the other three lodged in him. One in his right leg, arm, and neck. He was in and out of consciousness during the drive. I'm not sure how bad it is yet. I'll know that soon and I'll make sure to keep you posted.

"Damn, okay, we'll get on the first available flight in the morning."

"Okay, and maybe try not to tell Kenzie yet until we find out how he's really doing. He told me not to call her, but I had to at least call you, and I know y'all are close."

"Alright, I won't say anything," Lauren said before hanging up the phone.

I pulled Lauren close to me and she instantly broke down in tears. Blaze was her favorite cousin, so I was going to need him to pull through because if he didn't, I didn't know how Lauren or Kenzie would be able to deal with this.

"It's going to be alright, baby. Calm down and then get up and pack. I'll go online and look up some flights."

"Okay, do you think we should call your sister?"

"No, we told him we wouldn't and this isn't the kind of conversation to have with her over the phone. We'll go out there and see how everything is going, then I'll fly to Chicago and talk to her. I want to have all the details before I go out there and worry her."

"That's understandable, I just hope he pulls through. He

has a lot of people depending on him. Not to mention, I don't know how your sister will be able to handle this. I know that they aren't together anymore, but they both still love each other."

"I know they do and it'll work out for them. Blaze is tough and he's not going to go out without a fight," I assured her.

"Thank you, I needed to hear that. I love you so much," Lauren stated.

"I love you too," I replied before kissing her lips softly.

Lauren got up from the bed and pulled two suitcases from the closet. She started packing our things while I looked online for flights. They had a flight for 7 a.m., so I purchased three one-way tickets because I wasn't sure when we'd return. I put my phone back down and went into McKenna's room and packed her bag. By the time we were finished packing it was almost one in the morning. We laid in the bed and slept for a few hours before it was time for us to get up and head to the airport.

I woke my father up and told him what was going on before we left out and climbed in the awaiting car.

"Daddy, it's dark out here. I want to go back to bed," McKenna whined.

"I know, baby, it's early. You can sleep during this drive and when we get to the airport," I told her.

"Nooo, I want my bed, Daddy," she pouted.

I picked Kenna up from her seat and placed her on my lap. I held her and rocked her back to sleep. My baby was just like my sister. Her sleep was everything to her. If she didn't get her full eight hours of sleep, she'd wreak havoc and all of us would have to pay for it.

We made it to the airport thirty minutes later and went through TSA pre-check. We walked to our gate and sat down in a comfortable silence. I could tell that Lauren was trying her best to keep it together. I held her hand while I rocked McKenna back and forth. We stayed that way until it was time for us to board our flight.

As soon as we were in our seats, McKenna and Lauren passed out. We barely got sleep the night before and we had a five-and-a-half-hour flight ahead of us. I sent Mason a text letting him know what time we were landing before putting my phone on airplane mode. I turned a movie on but was halfway sleep before it was halfway done. By the time I woke up, our flight was beginning to land and McKenna was playing on her tablet.

Twenty-five minutes later, we were getting our luggage from the overhead bin and exiting the plane. I took my phone off airplane mode and saw a message from Mason letting me know a car would be outside waiting for us.

We walked through the busy airport and made our way outside. We looked around until we saw a guy holding a sign with my and Lauren's names on it. He helped us load our luggage into the trunk then we were on our way. I looked out the window during the drive, admiring the scenery. I loved Cali and wished we were here under better circumstances. I knew before we left, I had to take McKenna to Disneyland. This was her first time out here and I wanted her to be able to enjoy herself.

It took us about forty-five minutes before we pulled up to Mason and Blaze's mansion. It was about the same size as the one we lived in. The driver parked and got our bags out of the trunk. I tipped him then grabbed our bags. I rang the doorbell and after waiting a couple minutes, the door swung open.

"What's up, family, I can show you to your rooms so you can put your things away, then I'll take you down to see Blaze," Mason said.

"Wait, he's here? That means he's doing okay," Lauren beamed.

"No, he never went to the hospital. We brought him here and he's in our infirmary. You know we couldn't risk him going to a hospital. That would raise to many questions with the police. We have everything that any hospital has right downstairs, including surgeons on payroll and a nurse."

Lauren's smile fell before we followed Mason upstairs to our room. Lauren and I were sleeping in a guest bedroom and McKenna would be sleeping in Mason's daughter's room. They should be back in town later on that evening.

I got McKenna settled down in front of the TV, then Lauren and I went downstairs where Mason was waiting on us. We got on the elevator and took it down to the basement. We walked through a long hallway until we made it to a glass door. We walked inside and I had to say, I was impressed. I had an infirmary at my warehouse, but it didn't look shit like this. Had I not walked through the house and down to the basement, you wouldn't have been able to tell me this wasn't a hospital room.

The room was sterile and all white. It contained all the machines and equipment that could be found in a hospital. There was a machine and IV hooked up to Blaze. You could see all his vitals on the monitor. His right leg was elevated and there was a bandage on his neck and arm. Other than that, he looked like he was sleeping and breathing on his own. I was happy to at least see that part.

"How did things go with his surgery? Why isn't he woke yet?" Lauren asked.

"It went well, they were able to remove all the bullets, but he had lost a lot of blood and needed a transfusion. The bullet in his arm slid and entered his thorax with no exit wound. The one in his leg broke a bone, and the last one in his neck lodged close to the spine. They removed it, but they're not sure the impact that had yet until he wakes up. There's a possibility that he might be temporarily paralyzed. He will definitely have to undergo some major therapy when he wakes up," Mason informed us.

"Damn, how long do they expect him to be out?" I asked.

"We really don't know. It could be anything from a couple hours, to days, or even months," Mason replied.

As soon as the words left his mouth, Lauren broke down in tears. I sat in the chair next to Blaze's bed and pulled her down on my lap. I rocked her back and forth and she cried into my chest. We stayed that way for about thirty minutes until a girl came walking in the room with a bouquet of flowers and balloons. She sat them on the table then sat down on the other side of Blaze.

"Hey, I'm Blaze's girlfriend, Kim," she introduced herself.

Lauren's head shot up from my chest as she looked the girl up and down.

"Stop fucking lying, my cousin is not in a relationship with you."

"How are you going to tell me who I'm with? I never even seen you before."

"Yeah, and that should say a lot if you don't know who I am. I know all about you and you're on his payroll. Just because you're sucking his dick doesn't mean y'all in a relationship. You have to know you were only here to pass time. He's going to get back with McKenzie," Lauren pointed out.

"Baby, chill, now isn't the time for this," I whispered in Lauren's ear. Lauren was going to go to bat for McKenzie whether she was around to defend herself or not. I wasn't sure if the girl was with Blaze or not. I couldn't get mad if he was because he wasn't with McKenzie anymore and my sister wasn't an angel. I'm bias to the entire situation as long as he didn't put his hands on her or fuck her over.

I was pissed when I first found out he broke things off with my sister after sleeping with her, but he came to me as a man when he made it to Miami and explained everything to me. It all had to do with the timing being off. I could only honor the reasons why he left her. I respected him more for thinking about her safety over her feelings.

Kim looked at Lauren like she was about to say something, but Mason jumped in.

"Kim, let it go. You're not about to sit here and go back and forth with Lauren. We all know what you are to my brother. I appreciate everything that you've done for him and us, but she's family, so keep it cool before I have to ask you to leave."

"I'm sorry, you're right. I'm Blaze's special friend," she said with a smirk.

Lauren rolled her eyes and put her attention back on Blaze. She rubbed his hand and talked lowly so only he could hear what she was saying. We didn't know if he could hear us or not, but that didn't stop us from talking to him.

I stayed downstairs for about an hour then went back upstairs to spend time with McKenna. I was going to give it a few days before I hopped on a flight to go see McKenzie. There was no way I could go without telling her what's going on. She could hold a grudge, and the last thing I needed was for my sister to have to question my motives. I never was one to hide things from her, and I wasn't about to start now.

CHAPTER TWO
CHASE

When I finished taking care of business at the club I went straight home. I couldn't believe not only was Diane at a club, but she was there with some lame ass nigga. I knew I didn't have a right to be mad after the way I'd been treating her. Hell, I was barely even home as it was. She's smart and beautiful. There was only a matter of time before she got her lick back.

I parked in the driveway and walked inside of the dark house. I walked around and the only sound that could be heard were the heavy steps my feet made across the wooden floor. I walked into the bedroom we once shared together, and it was empty. There was no use for me to check the other rooms because I knew Diane wouldn't be in there.

This situation was funny to me because the roles were reversed and now I was the one sitting up waiting for her to come home. Then, to make matters worse, McKenzie was going to get in my ass. I hadn't seen my kids in almost three days. I'd been staying in the city at my old crib because I'd been busy making moves and getting my warehouse together. I promised her I was going to come by tonight to drop off some diapers and stuff for them. I knew they hadn't run out, but it's the point that I liked to keep my word when it came to the twins.

I pulled my phone out of my pocket and dialed McKenzie's number.

"Chase, it's almost two in the morning. What do you want?" McKenzie answered, sounding wide awake. I could hear music playing in her background and people laughing.

"Where are you and where are my kids?" I asked.

"None of your business. Had you came by earlier like you were supposed to, I might have told you."

I took the phone off my ear and took a deep breath. Diane and McKenzie were really trying my patience right now. I didn't want to take my anger out on Kenzie, but she was about to leave me no choice.

"Stop fucking playing with me, Kenzie. Where are my kids?"

Kenzie sighed before finally answering me.

"They're at home, where else would they be this time of night?"

"I would think they'd be with their mother."

"Well, you thought wrong. You're not the only parent that's allowed to go out and have fun. I work and take care of my kids all day, every day, so I deserved this break."

"Chill with that slick shit before I hit your ass in your mouth when I see you. Who's watching my kids?"

"I don't know who the fuck you think you talking to. You put your hands on me we gone be boxing. You know I don't play that shit. My mother is at the house with them."

"Okay, and where are you?"

"Nah, it don't work like that, playboy. I told you where the kids were and who they were with because you have the right to know. I, on the other hand, am not your concern. We're not in a relationship anymore. Just know I'm safe and so are your kids," she said before hanging up on me.

I couldn't help but laugh at what she'd just told me. She told me the same exact thing I was always telling Diane. I reminded her all the time that we're not in a relationship, and here I was tripping about seeing her with another man. I couldn't go out bad like this. The last thing I wanted her to see was me waiting up for her like some bitch after doing whatever with some other man.

I went upstairs to the bathroom and took a quick shower then got in bed. It was only a matter of minutes before I was passed out.

The following morning, I woke up and took care of my personal hygiene then got dressed in a pair of blue jeans and a white t-shirt with some Ones. I sprayed on cologne then grabbed my phone and walked downstairs to the kitchen. I looked at the clock and saw it was almost noon. I made a sandwich then grabbed some chips from the cabinet and a Pepsi from the fridge before walking into the living room. I sat on the couch and looked at my phone. I saw that McKenzie had called me twice. I pressed her number to return her call.

"Hello," McKenzie answered.

"Hey, you called me?"

"Yeah, are you going to buy the stuff for the kids today like you offered? They need diapers, wipes, toiletries, detergent, and formula. If you're not going to bring it today then let me know so I can go get it myself. I can't have my kids sitting around the house dirty."

I hated that she even had to call and ask me this. I was feeling like a dead-beat dad even though I came through for my kids financially. I was giving her more than what we agreed on but lately, I wasn't giving them as much time as I liked.

"I got the list you sent and I already bought everything from it. It's in my trunk along with some clothes I bought for them. I have to finish up something here then I'll be there to spend time with them. If you need anything else before I get there, let me know."

"You have until four o'clock, then I'm leaving and going to buy it myself," she told me before hanging up.

I was ready to say forget talking to Diane and just go to McKenzie's house but as quick as that idea came to mind, it left when the front door opened and closed.

Diane strolled in with the same clothes on from the night before and her messy hair pulled back into a ponytail.

"You had fun last night?" I asked, looking up at her.

"Yep, I imagine just as much fun as you have with McKenzie when you're fucking her," she replied sarcastically.

Before I could catch myself, I jumped up from the couch and slammed Diane into the wall.

"Watch your motherfucking mouth before I show you another side of me. Don't forget whose house this is and who pays all the god damn bills in this bitch. You got some new dick and getting beside yourself. You gone have to call that nigga and tell him to come pick your ass up off this floor."

"Ouch, get off of me," Diane winced.

"How do you know him and how long have y'all been fucking? You better not have been bringing him in my house."

"I work with him, and yesterday was the first time we went out. It was a group of us that went to the club together. I just so happened to have left with him. He's never been in this house before. I would never do that, no matter how mad I am at you."

"Look, I gave this some thought last night. We're not together anymore so you're free to do whatever you like. I just don't want to see or hear about the shit. If I ever catch y'all in my house, I'm going to shoot both of you," I warned her as I took a few steps backward.

A look of relief spread across her face, then it was followed by dread and sorrow.

"It's really over between us, isn't it? I know you, and you're being too understanding right now. Since we're being honest, I need you to be honest with me for a change. You're back sleeping with Kenzie?"

"I can't say what will happen in the future but right now, I can't give you what you want and need. I tried, but I just can't do it. I still love McKenzie and we've been sleeping together. I owe it to her and my kids to try and give them a family. The only way she'll take me seriously is if I'm not living under the same roof as you. I'm going to move back to my old house and you can stay here for as long as you need."

"How could you do this to me, Chase? You wasted all these years with me only to leave me for another girl. Did you ever really love me?"

"Yeah, I did, you were my best friend. I'm starting to realize that maybe I never loved you the same way you did me and for that, I'm sorry. I never meant to hurt you."

"Whatever, Chase, you could have been told me this shit when we first started fucking around. I can't believe I was this damn stupid and put up with all your bullshit. Just do whatever the hell you want. I'll start looking for a place and be out of your hair soon so you can move your family in here," she said before storming away.

I walked up the stairs behind Diane but instead of saying anything else to her, I grabbed a duffle bag from the closet and stuffed some clothes in it. I had hygiene stuff at my house and Kenzie's, so I didn't need to grab that. Once I was done, I sat on the bed next to Diane.

"You don't have to rush and move out. I never said any of

those things to hurt you. You asked for the truth and that was the least I could do. You'll always have a spot in my heart. The timing is just off with us right now. If you need anything, call me."

I waited a couple minutes and when she didn't say anything, I grabbed my bag and left the room.

I never meant to hurt Diane, but it was time for me to stop lying. McKenzie was single and so was I. There's nothing in the way of us finally being together. I was going to go over to her house and let her know I ended things with Diane for good and I was moving out.

I left the house and climbed in my car. I drove straight to McKenzie's house. I parked next to Tori's car in the driveway. I grabbed the kids' stuff from my trunk then walked up to McKenzie's door. I rang the doorbell and waited for someone to answer. I left her house key on her nightstand the day she went off on me for using a key.

Tori opened the door for me and we spoke as I entered the house. Kenzie was sitting on the floor playing with the twins. I looked down at them and smiled. I took my shoes off and joined them on the floor. My princess crawled over and sat on my lap.

"Hey, daddy's baby, you missed me? Because I missed you, your brother, and mommy too."

McKenzie looked up at me and rolled my eyes before getting up from the floor with my son.

"It's time for their nap, bring her up to bed," McKenzie said.

I followed McKenzie up the stairs and we put the kids in the crib. The good thing about the twins was their bodies were on a schedule. If we stuck to it, they didn't cause us any problems. They didn't even have to get rocked to sleep often. All we had to do was turn on the mobile over their crib and they were fast asleep.

McKenzie turned on the baby monitor then left the room. We walked to her room and she laid across the bed.

"Are you cooking tonight? If not, I can order dinner."

"I was going to cook, but if you want to buy me food I'll gladly eat it." She smiled.

"You have my card information. You can order whatever you want when you're ready."

"Okay, thank you."

"You're welcome. You know you can thank me by letting me put you to sleep," I said as I raised my eyebrows.

"We haven't had sex in almost a week. You mean to tell me you ain't get no pussy while you were away?"

"No, I haven't. I've been working these last few days. I stayed at home last night but Diane wasn't there. I ended things with her today and told her I was moving out. I want to give us another shot. I want to do things the right way this time, if you let me."

McKenzie looked me in the eyes after I finished talking. I guess she was trying to see if I was telling the truth or not.

"I don't know, Chase. I need to think about this first. If it doesn't work between us, I don't want it or affect our kids."

"I get where you're coming from, but baby, we owe it to our kids to do things the right way. Just give me a chance and I promise I'll do whatever it takes to show you how much I love you."

"Okay, but this is your only shot and we're not together yet. I need to make sure I can trust you first."

"Alright, I understand, and I'll wait for as long as you need me to," I told her before leaning in and kissing her on the lips.

McKenzie welcomed the kiss and before I knew it, we were

both out of our clothes and my tongue was dipping inside of her honey pot. I devoured her pussy until she was coming all over my face. She grabbed a condom from her nightstand and handed it to me. I grumbled before putting it on. I hated wearing condoms when we had sex, but that was the only way she was going to give me some. I hadn't had sex with her raw since the twins were born.

I slid inside of her and she immediately wrapped her legs around me, allowing me to go in as deep as I could. Her shit was soaking wet and I was trying my best not to bust quick. We fucked for a good thirty minutes until I was pulling the condom off and busting on her ass.

We caught our breath then took a shower and got dressed. After that, Kenzie ordered some food and we went downstairs to watch a movie while we waited.

I pulled McKenzie into my arms and kissed the top of her forehead. This was all that I ever wanted from the beginning. I could finally see us being happy together. I was going to do my best to make sure that McKenzie could feel the love I had for her.

CHAPTER THREE
BLAZE

I 'd been trying to open my eyes for God knows how long. I wasn't sure how long I'd been out of it. All I knew was that I was shot, but I wasn't sure when or what damage had been done. I wasn't sure if I was going to make it that day. The pain that was coursing through my body was indescribable. I had never felt this much pain in my life. I was in and out of consciousness when I was carried out of the warehouse and into the back of a truck.

My brother was barking orders over the phone the entire time he sped away from the warehouse. He was telling Kim to keep me woke and she was talking, but it was hard for me keep my eyes open or focus on what she was saying. I was tired of fighting and all I wanted to do was sleep. I couldn't handle the pain anymore.

It didn't take Mason long to get me to our house. I already knew that's where they were going to bring me. We had the best doctors on payroll that money could buy. Sadly, we used them more often than we liked.

As soon as they brought me into the infirmary, Rafael and his team got straight to work. My clothes were cut off and my wounds were assessed. I opened my mouth and tried to speak, but words wouldn't come out. It felt like I was drowning in my own blood. After that, they hurriedly connected me to an IV. I wasn't sure what was in it, but I could no longer hear what anyone in the room was saying. The more they talked the further away they sounded and before I knew it, I had faded away. I didn't know if it was from the drugs or if I was dying, but I hadn't been able to open my eyes since.

Come on, you can do this. Just open your eyes, I willed myself.

I finally opened my eyes but immediately closed them back. There was a bright light shining and my eyes needed to adjust to them. I waited a couple minutes then opened them again. I turned my head slightly and saw my little sister's big head ass lying on my arm. I looked to the other side and Kim was right there.

"Kendra," I whispered unintentionally. My voice was hoarse so my words were coming out low. My throat felt like I had been eating sandpaper for breakfast lunch and dinner.

My sister didn't hear me, so I lifted my arm and she jumped.

"Oh my god, Kai, you're finally woke. You scared the hell out of us," Kendra beamed with tears in her eyes.

"How long have I been out?" I asked lowly.

"You've been in a coma-like state for almost two weeks now. Mom was scared Rafael had messed up your surgery. She was trying to get Mason to take you to the hospital but he wouldn't. They assured Mama that it was normal due to the injuries you sustained.

"I need some water, my throat is on fire," I told her.

Kendra got up from her seat and walked over to the refrigerator. She grabbed a cup and put some ice in it then brought it over to me.

"Here, eat the ice, I'm not sure if you can have water yet. I'll text Mason and let him know you're awake. One of the nurses will come in and check on you until Rafael makes it."

I took the cup from Kendra and put a couple ice cubes in my mouth. They immediately soothed my throat, so I put more in my mouth before trying to speak again.

"How bad are my injuries?" I asked, a bit clearer now.

"You were hit six times. Three to the vest and three flesh wounds. You lost a lot of blood before they got you here and they had to give you a transfusion. The bullet in your neck was close to your spine, so Rafael said he's not sure what the damage that's done yet. Your right leg has a cast on it because one of the bones is broken, and your right arm and neck are bandaged because bullets were removed from there as well."

I was about to respond when Kim opened her eyes and looked at me.

"Baby, you're awake. Don't ever scare me like this again," Kim told me before jumping on top of me kissing me all over my face. I wanted to push her away but I didn't have the strength.

A few minutes passed before people walked into the room. I couldn't tell who it was because Kim's body was blocking the way.

"Get your dumb ass off of him. I know you see he's bandaged up and just woke up," I heard Lauren say. I tried to contain my smile because she said everything I was thinking.

Kim scoffed before moving so Lauren could take her place. Lauren leaned over and hugged me gently then kissed me on the forehead.

"What's up, troublemaker?" I asked.

"Nothing, was waiting for you to wake up so I could kick your ass."

"Kick my ass for what? I haven't done anything."

"Yeah, you did, but I'm going to give you time to heal before I get in your ass," Lauren threatened me.

"Kim, I'm hungry. Can you go find me some soup or a sandwich?"

"Sure, baby, I'll be back as soon as possible," she said before walking away.

Once Kim was out of earshot, I responded to Lauren.

"Damn, I just woke up and I'm already getting threatened. You're here by yourself?"

"No, Tez and Kenna are here with me. He's putting her to bed for me then he'll be down," Lauren answered.

"How long have y'all been here?"

"Mason called me the night you were shot, and we came straight out here the next morning."

"Did y'all tell McKenzie?"

"No, Mason didn't want to tell her over the phone, but he's going to Chicago to tell her. He was just waiting for you to wake up first."

"I told Mason not to tell her."

"Mason didn't tell her, but you can't expect us not to tell her. If it was up to me, she would have found out the same night I did. You're wrong for keeping this from her just like other stuff. If you weren't ready for a relationship, you should have just told her that."

"What are you talking about? McKenzie knows why we aren't together."

"Bullshit, you told me the reason you weren't, but that didn't stop you from getting back with Kim."

"I'm not with no damn Kim. I've never been in a relationship with that girl. She's just here passing time. I planned on going back to Chicago after the mission was completed that day and getting my girl back."

"Okay, so what's your plan now?"

"I'm still going to try and get her back, but I have to wait now. I can't even get up out of this damn bed let alone hop on a plane and go to her."

Lauren sighed before sitting in the seat next to me.

"You can still talk to her on the phone and tell her what's going on."

"I mean, I could, but I'm not. She'll only jump on a plane and come out here. I want her to get back with me because she wants me. Not because she feels bad for me."

"So that means you're just going to continue to fuck Kim until then?" Lauren inquired.

"I'm not going to be fucking anybody. Hell, I don't even know if my shit gone get hard. I have to focus on getting better first and right now, I'm fucked up. I'm out of commission for at least the next two months now."

Lauren sat back in her seat, deep in thought. I could tell she was debating on going on with the subject, but I didn't want to talk about it anymore. Just thinking about the shit pissed me off.

Lauren finally opened her mouth to say something, but she closed it right back when Mason walked in the room.

"What's up, lil' bro, how are you feeling?" Mason asked.

"Like my ass been shot up," I replied, serious. Now that I was woke, the pain medication felt like it was wearing off.

"Rafael is almost here. He told us not to give you any more medication because it might put you to sleep, but he needs to examine you while you're awake first."

"It's cool, I'll deal with the pain. I'm just happy to still be alive."

"Man, me too. Mama would have sent me to be with you had you not made it out of there alive."

"Where is she anyway?"

"She had some errands to run, but she's been here every day by your side. I called her and she should be here in about an hour."

"Okay, did you call Tamika and Tasia?"

"Yeah, Tasia is actually here. She came with Ciara and the kids the day after it happened. Tamika's flight will be here this evening. She already had the flight scheduled."

"Good, I missed the hell out of my kids."

I talked to Mason and Lauren for a little while until Tez came in. He had a look on his face I couldn't decipher.

"What's going on? I'm glad you're finally up. You had my woman and your family stressed out," Tez finally said.

"Shit, believe me, I didn't intend on getting caught slipping. Somebody didn't make sure the area was completely clear, but it's cool though. I'm still grateful as hell. If I wouldn't have had that vest on, y'all would have been at my funeral by now."

"True, and if it was up to you, my sister would never know."

There it goes. I knew Tez wasn't going to have a full conversation with me without bringing up Kenzie.

"It's not that I don't want McKenzie to know. Things are complicated between us and if she drops everything and comes here now, it won't change much because I can't go back there yet and she can't stay here. Plus, I'm not trying to put her in an uncomfortable situation. Both Tasia and Kim are here right now. I'm going to call her, though, and once I'm better, I'll meet up with her," I explained.

"Are you going to tell her you were shot?"

"I'm still debating on that. I don't want to tell her over the phone and worry her."

"It's cool, because I'm going to tell her tomorrow when I fly out there. You know how Kenzie is and I'm not going to keep this from her any longer. You might be fine with her being mad and not talking to you, but I'm not. I'll do anything for my sister to make sure she's happy, and I can't go without her talking to me."

I took in everything Tez was saying to me, and he was right. I hated keeping things from Kenzie, but I guess I didn't know how to tell her I'd been shot but not to come here. I didn't want to be proving her right about why I called things off between us. I really did leave her just to keep her safe. Tasia and Kim just so happened to be there to pass time. The way I looked at it, I was able to make sure everyone was safe with the way things went. I was going to make things right with Kenzie as soon as I was able to get up out of this bed. I was going to call her tonight, though, because there's no telling what's been going through her mind since our last conversation. I told her I love her and hadn't contacted her back since. I knew she probably thought I was on some bullshit. I had to at least tell her something before she ended up fed up with my shit for good.

Everyone hung around until Rafael finally showed up and performed my examination. Everything seemed to be healing properly, but there was some numbness in my right arm and my right leg didn't have much sensation in it. I knew this the moment I woke up, but I didn't want to worry my family. Rafael tried to assure me that it was normal and once I was up and moving around, there was a chance that it would return.

I'm trying to be optimistic about the situation, but I'm not too sure. I never imagined myself not getting around on my own. He suggested I stay down here on bedrest for at least another week before I could move around or attempt to start physical therapy. Thinking about the process I had to go through to get back to normal sounded worse than me actually being shot. I didn't have much of anything to worry about, though, because I had more than enough help to look out for me while I was here. All of this was just fucked up on so many levels.

Since I was alone, I decided to call McKenzie now and get it over with. The phone rang three times before she finally picked up.

"Hello," she answered.

My words were caught in my throat from hearing her voice. I didn't know how this conversation was going to go.

"Hey, how are you doing?"

"How am I doing? Are you serious, Blaze? You call me last week out of the blue telling me how much you missed me and the kids. Claiming that you love me and want me to forgive you when it's all over, but then you disappear all over again."

I knew Kenzie was going to be pissed but not this pissed. This was the first time she ever called me Blaze, and I hated it. She was special and had the right to call me by my actual name.

"I'm sorry, Kenz, I meant everything I said that day. Everything was coming to an end and I was prepared to come back to Chicago the next day to see you."

"Then why aren't we having this conversation in person?" she asked, interrupting me.

I paused for a moment to decide if I was going to tell her or not. I knew that I might as well because Tez was going to tell her when he made it out there.

"I was shot that same night, and I just woke up today."

"Oh my god, are you alright?"

"Yeah, I'll be alright. I got shot in the leg, arm, and neck.

I'm on bedrest right now until my wounds heal more, then I'll have to undergo physical therapy."

"I'm sorry to hear that, is there anything I can do?"

"Nah, I'm good, I just need you to be a little more patient for me," I told her.

"Okay, maybe I can come out there and see you. I can bring the twins to see you as well."

This was exactly why I didn't want to tell her. Now I was about to piss her off all over again with the answer I was about to give her.

"I would love for you to come out here, but right now isn't a good time. Kim and Tasia are here and I don't want to make you uncomfortable."

"Wow, so you've been fucking both of them while we weren't together. I wish you were man enough to tell me the real reason why you wanted to break up. You're no better than Chase's ass and you tried to prove how wrong he was for me. Don't even fuckin' bother calling me when you're better. Lose my number and don't send shit else to me or my kids," McKenzie snapped before hanging up on me. I called her right back, but she didn't answer the phone.

"Fuck!" I yelled before throwing my phone across the room.

Lauren and Kim ran in the room after hearing me scream.

"Are you alright, baby?" Kim asked, running over to me.

"Yeah, I just need some time to myself," I told her calmly, trying to contain my anger. None of this was her fault, but looking at her was pissing me off.

Kim turned and stormed out of the room, leaving me alone with Lauren and Kendra.

"What happened?" Lauren inquired.

"I just got off the phone with Kenzie and I told her everything. She told me not to contact her again and hung up on me."

"Damn, just give her some time to calm down. Tez will talk to her tomorrow, and she'll come around soon."

"I wish it was that simple, but we both know it's not going to be that easy this time," I said before closing my eyes. I could feel a headache coming on. I had truly fucked up this time and I didn't know what to do about it. All I could do now was focus on getting better and fight like hell to get Kenzie to forgive me in the end.

CHAPTER FOUR
MCKENZIE

Malakai's timing was always fucking off. I was about to put his ass on the block list because every time I talked to him, he fucked up my mood. He brought back too many feelings that I didn't want to feel. This shit wasn't fair to me at all, and I didn't think he realized what he was doing to me.

I walked back into the living room and picked up the Patrón so I could pour me another drink. I was having a good night until his dumb ass called and ruined it. Tori, Charmaine, and I were in middle of our girls' night. We had just finished our pedicures and were in the middle of drinking and listening to music while having girl talk, until Malakai had called. We were all talking about our relationship issues and now I had even more shit to get off my chest.

I poured two shots of Patrón and knocked them both back. Typically, I wouldn't even be drinking like this when the twins were home, but they were in bed already and their father should be here in a couple hours. Ever since Chase asked for us to get back together, he'd been here every night making sure me and the twins were good. He even got up early in the morning and allowed me to sleep while he fed and changed them. I still hadn't given him an definitive answer yet, but I saw all the effort he was making. I was trying not to think about what happened in the past and start over fresh, but that's hard to do when a person hurt you the way Chase hurt me.

If it wasn't for my twins, I wouldn't have anything to do with Chase though. I never would have even been close to forgiving his lying, cheating ass. Part of me wanted to forgive him and say what the hell, let's be a family, but then the other side was like fuck this love bullshit. Especially with how things were going between me and Malakai.

"Slow down, Kenzie, are you alright?" Charmaine asked, pulling me away from my thoughts.

"No, I'm not," I said honestly as tears started to fall from my eyes.

"Awww, baby, don't cry. Do you want to talk about it?" Tori inquired.

"It's Malakai, he's such a dumb ass. I told y'all how he wanted me to forgive him and that he should be on his way back out here. Well, come to find out, he was shot that same night and just woke up today. I offered to go see him and the nigga had the nerve to tell me it wasn't a good idea since Tasia and Kim were there. Now, don't get me wrong, it's understandable that Tasia would be there because she's his baby mama, but that bitch Kim is a different story. He got me thinking he's fucking both of them and that's why he broke up with me."

"Girl, niggas are stupid, but you know Blaze isn't like that. I'm sure he ended things for the reasons he said, but at the same time, they're both convenient for him while he's not with you. Kind of how things are between you, Chase, and Liam. You still want to have your fun but you don't want to start with anyone new. I mean, you could have easily went out and started dating someone else, but part of you is holding out for Blaze," Charmaine pointed out.

As bad as I didn't want to admit it, Charmaine was right. I could tell my girls that, but I'd never let Malakai know that, and I wasn't ready to forgive him yet.

"You're right, but it's still fucked up how all of this is turning out. I'm torn between Malakai and Chase. I don't know what to do or who to be with." I sighed as I plopped down on the couch.

"It's a part of growing up. You don't have to rush into anything. Especially if it involves getting back with Chase. I see him being here for his kids and I'll never knock him for that. He's amazing with them and it looks like he's trying to make you happy, but that doesn't take away from all that he's done. You're my girl and you know I'll always have your back, but I want you to really sit down and think about what you want to do. Don't choose to be with Chase just because you're mad at Malakai. You're beautiful and there's plenty of guys out there besides them two. You don't have to be with either of them. We'll make sure you and the kids are well taken care of," Tori added.

This right here was why she's my best friend. She had my back regardless and wouldn't sugar coat shit with me. She saw things that I didn't see myself.

"I love you ladies and I'm grateful to have both you in my life. Now enough of this mushy shit. Let's drink and enjoy the rest of our night," I said.

"We love you too, now bottoms up, bitches," Charmaine laughed.

We continued to drink and enjoy the rest of our night until Chase showed up a couple hours later. He spoke, kissed me on the forehead, then went straight up to my room so he wouldn't disturb us. By the time we finished, it was almost two in the morning and I was nice and tipsy. Tori and Charmaine went up to Tori's room and I went up to mine where Chase was in bed knocked out sleep.

I stripped out of my clothes and climbed into bed with him. He was butt ass naked like always. Chase never slept in clothes when he was in the bed with me. Typically, I would at least have a t-shirt on, but not tonight. I was drunk and horny, so that meant I was on a mission to get some dick before I went to sleep. I ran kisses down Chase's collar bone while I stroked his semi-erect manhood.

"If you trying to fuck you gone have to do all the work. I'm tired as shit," Chase mumbled.

"I can deal with that," I replied before straddling him and sliding down on his dick.

Chase claimed I would have to do all the work, but it was only a matter of time until he was fucking me back, making me cum on his dick. That wasn't enough for him, so he flipped over onto my stomach and hit it from the back, unleashing the beast.

Chase was tired and I was drunk as hell, so neither of us had much energy. We were both cumming ten minutes later. Normally I would be pissed that it was so short, but I came twice and I really did need some sleep so I would have energy to be up with my kids later on. He pulled me close to him and kissed me on my forehead. We stayed in that position until we both fell asleep.

Later on that day, I woke up in an empty bed. I looked over at the clock and saw it was noon. I couldn't believe I had slept that long. I climbed out of bed and went into the bathroom. I brushed my teeth then climbed in the shower. I was glad that Chase allowed me to sleep because I didn't have a hangover.

When I finished my shower, I grabbed some underwear

from my drawer and put them on along with a pair of leggings and a half shirt. I brushed my hair into a ponytail and put on a pair of socks. I wasn't planning on leaving out today. Sundays were my lazy day, which consisted of me cooking, cleaning, studying, and doing laundry. By the time I finished getting dressed and situated, an hour passed.

I walked down the stairs and found Chase sitting on the couch with my brother. I ran over, and my brother embraced me in a big hug.

"Hey, I'm about to go to the city to take care of some business. I'll be back later on. If you need anything, give me a call," Chase said. He leaned over and kissed me gently on the lips and I returned the kiss. He kissed both of the babies then was out of door.

"You're back with him?" Martez asked.

"It's complicated. What are you doing here though? I wasn't expecting to see you until December when I came down there."

"I came today so I could check on you and the twins. I'm staying for a couple days then I have to go back to Cali to meet up with Lauren and McKenna."

"How long were you in Cali?"

"We been there for about a week now. We're staying there for one more week."

"So you knew Malakai was shot and didn't tell me?"

"I found out the night it happened. He didn't want you to know at first. I said I'd wait and see how he was doing and if he woke up first before I came out here. I wanted to at least give you some good news first. I told him to call and tell you what happened or I was going to. Did he call you?"

"Yeah, his dumb ass did. He told me everything, including the fact that Tasia and Kim are there," I said as I flopped down on the couch.

"Okay, in his defense, I don't think he's with neither one of them. Yeah, he might have been sleeping with them, but that's about it. You already know how that go."

"Really, Tez? So I'm just supposed to be fine with this? He broke up with me because he claimed he wanted to keep me safe. I'd prefer if he would have kept it real with me from beginning."

"He was honest with you, Kenzie. They were in some real deep shit out here. Hell, him getting shot should prove his point. You weren't safe being with him. Everything he did was to keep you safe. I know you hate that he was with them again, but imagine how he'll feel knowing that you've started up a relationship with Chase again. Would you have rather he moved on and found someone else new or slept around with random women? I would think that would be worse than what he's done."

"Ugh, I hate that you're right. That doesn't mean I'm not still mad at him though. I know the timing is just fucked up, but I can't keep going back and forth with him. I'd rather him just contact me once he's done with all this bullshit and ready to sit down and talk. I can't promise I'll still be single at the time, but I can at least say we'll be on good terms."

"That's understandable, and if it's meant to be then it'll happen for you two again. I'm pretty sure he didn't just stay by your side over a year just to sleep with them. He told me everything when he came to Miami. I'm a good judge of character, and that man really does love you the same way that you love him."

"I know he loves me, I don't question that. I just wish it could be easier. Everything was falling into place with my life, now it's like I'm back at square one."

"You're not at square one. At the end of the day, no matter what happens, you have those twins to be strong for. You're beautiful with money and a roof over your head. You just got promoted with your job. You're stable, baby girl, and you can make it without either of those niggas in your lives. You're my sister and at the end of the day, I'm going to always be on your side. You're more important than any business deal. I don't care if he's Lauren's cousin or not. I'll fuck him up for you if you want me to," Martez said with a straight face.

I laughed gently because I knew Martez was serious. We sat around and talked a little while longer and played with the twins until I got up and started on dinner. I was making lamb chops, asparagus, and scallop potatoes. Tori left to go over her boyfriend's house, so it was just me, Martez, and the twins.

I loved having my brother around. Sometimes I debated on moving back to Miami, but I always changed my mind when I realized they would have to grow up without their father, and then there's my mother to think about as well. She'd been very hands on when it came to the twins. She came through to babysit whenever I needed her to and sometimes, she came without me even having to ask her. I didn't let them go to her house, though, because I didn't trust Ricky. If he did something stupid with my kids in the house, I'd put a bullet in his ass myself. My mother claimed that he didn't hit her anymore, but I didn't know how true that was. All I could do was take her word for it.

I finished cooking dinner and we sat down and ate. After dinner, Martez cleaned the kitchen while I bathed and put the kids to bed. Once I was done, I took a shower then joined Martez in the living room to watch a movie. I was tired so I went upstairs to go bed as soon as the movie was over, leaving Martez downstairs on his own.

I tossed and turned in bed, thinking about what everyone had told me. I was torn between two men and being single. This decision would be easier if I didn't love them both. I loved them for different reasons and if I'm being honest, I didn't trust either one of them with my heart right now, but at the same time, I didn't want to leave them alone. I still couldn't believe somehow, I ended up in a fucking love triangle. Thinking about it was giving me a headache, so I finally closed my eyes and was able to go to sleep.

CHAPTER FIVE
DIANE

I'd been online looking for a house for the past week but hadn't been able to find anything. Chase had me spoiled with this house and there was no way I could afford anything like this. I would settle for an apartment like the one I moved out of but there's none available right now.

I'm not trying to live from paycheck to paycheck. I'd never done that before. I think that's why I put up with so much of Chase's shit because I never had to struggle financially. He's always been a provider for me and I barely touched my own money unless I wanted to.

I still couldn't believe that Chase actually moved out for real. He's made that threat before but he never stood on it. I guess he really was done this time. He lied about where he was going to stay though. I drove by his old house a few times and his car was never there. I knew that it could be because he's out handling business, but his car wasn't out there during the day time or night time.

I was sitting here stuck, so I decided to call Chase's mother. The phone rang twice before she picked up.

"Hey daughter, how are you doing?"

"Hey Ma, not so good."

"What has my knuckle-headed son done now?" Juliet asked as she sighed into the phone. I could tell she was tired of our shit, but I had no one else to talk to about this. "We got into a really bad fight because I slipped up and slept with someone else. It didn't mean anything to me. I was just mad at how he had been treating me and I was lonely. He packed up some of his things and told me he was moving back to his old house. He admitted that he was sleeping with Kenzie again and that the only way he would get a chance to be there as a family with her is if I wasn't in the picture," I explained as tears fell from my eyes.

"When did all of this take place?"

"It's been about a week now. He's not answering my calls and he hasn't been back to the house."

"Look, you know that I love you like I love my boys. I can understand how you slept with someone else. A person can only take so much of somebody's bullshit before they do something out of the ordinary. I haven't seen Chase none this week so he's not staying in his old house. When I do talk to him, he's out in the streets or with his kids, so I'm assuming that he's staying with Kenzie. I still don't like her but she is the mother of my grandkids, who I love dearly. At the end of the day, you have to do what's best for you, Diane. If you think being with my son is what's best, then you need to let the man you slept with know that it was a mistake and it will never happen again. After that, you have to get off your ass and do what it takes to get Chase to come back home. On the other hand, if being with Chase isn't what you really want, you have to let him go and you both move on with your life. Whatever your decision is, you'll still be like a daughter to me and you can call and come around whenever you like."

I listened closely to what Juliet was telling me. She was right about everything she was saying. Since my own mother wasn't around, she'd always been a mother figure to me.

"I know I sound crazy, but I'm not ready to give up on Chase yet. I still love him and I haven't shown him how much he's been appreciated lately."

"You're not crazy, baby, you're just in love. You know what you need to do, so get off this phone and do what you need to do in order to get your man back."

"Thank you for always being here. I'll call you in a couple days with an update."

"You don't have to thank me, and I'll be waiting for your call," Juliet said before hanging up the phone.

I sat back in my seat thinking about the conversation Juliet and I just had. Justin was a cool guy, but I wasn't willing to open my heart up to him after being in a relationship with Chase all these years. I didn't know what skeletons were in his closet. At least with Chase, I knew what I was getting myself into. I knew him and I knew what he liked and disliked.

I told Chase that I was going to accept his kids, but all I did was bitch and push him right back into Kenzie's bed. I could admit that I'm partially to blame for what's taking place between us. I hadn't given my all to this relationship since the day I found out she was pregnant. I'd just been going with the motion. I knew that I had to show Chase that I really wanted him to be with me or it'd never work between us. I'd allowed to much shit to slide and it ended now. I knew it'd be hard to compete with his kids, but I'm willing to take extreme measures. The first thing I was going to do was go to Justin's house and talk to him. It's only right that I had this conversation face to face.

I got up from the couch and threw on a black PINK jogging suit and some sneakers since I'd been lounging around the house all day with one of Chase's shirts on. I combed my hair into a messy ponytail then grabbed my keys and purse. Normally, I wouldn't go to a person's house unannounced, but I needed to do this now while I had the courage. I didn't want things to be awkward between us when I went to work tomorrow. We'd been flirting all week at work but we never discussed what happened again, so I didn't even know if Justin wanted a relationship or I was just a quick fuck.

I pulled up to Justin's condo and parked next to his car. I took a deep breath before climbing out of the car. I rang the doorbell and waited until I heard Justin's voice over the intercom.

"Who is it?" he called out.

"Diane," I answered.

Justin hit the buzzer and I walked into the building. His door was already opened so I walked in. Justin was standing by the refrigerator in nothing but his boxers, drinking a bottle of water. Water was glistening on his skin, so I could tell he had just gotten out of the shower. I had to get my hormones in control so I could have this conversation with him. I was ready to say fuck it and let him have his way with me right here on his island.

"Well, this is a nice surprise. What brings you over this way?"

"I came over because we needed to talk about what happened last week so that we're not tip toeing around it."

"Okay, what's up, let's talk."

"I like you and I really enjoyed myself that night, but it can't happen again. I'm not going to say it was a mistake, but I'm just not in the right head space to start something new with you. I'm not completely over my ex yet and I still live in his house. I need to figure out what I want to do with my life and I don't feel comfortable leading you on in the process."

"I hear you and I understand where you're coming from. I didn't want to rush into anything either. I just wanted to see where things can go with us. I just got out of a two-year relationship a couple months ago and if I'm being honest, I'm not sure where I stand with her. I'm cool with us being friends. We can have sex every now and then if you want. It can be our secret. I'm not trying to disrupt what you have going on."

"Alright, I'm glad that we're on the same page. I won't hold you up though. I have another run to make before I go home."

"Okay, see you tomorrow," Justin said.

I left Justin's house and put Kenzie's address in my GPS. I found her address one day when I was snooping through Chase's things. I'd never been to her house before but I was desperate now. Maybe if I had an actual conversation with her, she'd understand where I was coming from and end things with Chase for good.

It took me thirty minutes to get to Kenzie's house from Justin's. I was in awe as I pulled up to the front of her house. The landscape of her house was breathtaking, and it was bigger than the house Chase and I shared. Seeing this just made me green with envy. I didn't know exactly how much Chase was giving her, but it had to be a nice amount of money for her to afford this house. There was a black BMW parked in the driveway and Chase's car was nowhere in sight. That didn't mean he wasn't here, though, because his car could be parked in her garage.

I had come this far, so there was no turning back now. I climbed out of the car and rang her doorbell. I stood there for about a minute until I heard a guy's voice say who is it. I gave my name and there was a little bit of shuffling until the front door finally opened.

I was surprised to see this fine ass man open the door. He was tall with a light caramel complexion, dreamy eyes, and wavy hair. I stood there looking at him for I don't know how long until he snapped his fingers in my face.

"What do you want?" he all but yelled in my face.

"I'm sorry, is Chase here?" I asked.

"Chase doesn't live here, so you can leave now," he said rudely.

"Okay, well is Kenzie here? I really need to talk to her for a minute."

I heard him yell for Kenzie, and she came down to door holding one of the twins in her arms. She handed the baby to him and he whispered something in her ear before walking away.

"What the hell are you doing at my house?" McKenzie yelled.

"I'm sorry, I just thought that we should finally talk to face to face. That's something that we haven't done yet and I think it's well overdue."

"What could we possibly have to talk about?"

"We need to talk about you and Chase. He moved out because he wants to be there for you and the kids. He told me that he wants to be a family with you, but I can't lie and say that I don't still love him. I've known Chase since I was a child. He and his family are that all that I know I have. I think it's time for you to step back and just allow him to be there for his kids. I know that you don't love him the way that I do."

McKenzie looked at me with a straight face before she started busting out into laughter.

"Bitch, I know you didn't come to my house calling yourself marking your territory. Chase is here because this is where he wants to be. I didn't ask him to leave you and come to me. He did that all on his own. He's the one begging me to give him another chance. That should tell you a lot. I'm the wrong person to be having this conversation with. I can call Chase for you if you like and you can tell him all of this. Not that it would make a difference. I'm going to give you some advice. Stop wasting your time and let it go. Even if I'm not with him, you should still let it go because that means he's just settling for you. You're a pretty girl and I'm sure there's someone else out there for you. Also, let this be the last time you show up at my house. The next time I won't be so understanding," she told me before slamming the door in my face.

I couldn't believe she was giving me attitude when I came over talking to her nicely. There was still more that I needed to say and I wasn't leaving until I got it off my chest. I lifted my fist and started banging on her door. She snatched it open, and the look on her face made me rethink my choice of knocking on her door again.

"I wasn't done talking to you," I said.

"I don't motherfucking care if you were done talking or not. I don't owe you shit and I gave you a nice piece of advice. I told you what your friends should be telling you. You don't just show up at somebody's house like this. I could have beat the shit out of you the moment my brother opened the door for you because I find you showing up at my house as being disrespectful."

"I didn't come over here to disrespect you. That wasn't my intentions at all. I just didn't know what else to do. You and Chase have left me in a bad position. I basically have to find a place of my own and start over from scratch."

Kenzie was about to respond to me, but Chase stopped her when he walked up behind her. I'm assuming he parked in her garage and entered through the back door.

"Go upstairs with our kids. I'll take care of this," Chase told her. Kenzie did as she was told without giving me a second look.

"What the hell are you doing here, Diane? Take your ass

home and don't come back here again," Chase bellowed. Chase had never yelled at me like this before. My soft ass was ready to break down in tears.

"I came over to talk to Kenzie. I want you to come back home, Chase. I love you and I'm not ready to give up on us."

"I'm not trying to hear this shit. Go home and I'll stop by one day this week," Chase said before closing the door in my face.

I was going to knock on the door again, but I didn't want to piss Chase off any more, so I walked to my car and got in. The tears I was holding instantly fell from my eyes. I tried, so now the ball was in his court. There was nothing left for me to do except go home and drown in my own sorrows until Chase came around.

CHAPTER SIX

CHASE

I couldn't believe Diane's dumb ass showed up here. I didn't even know how she got Kenzie's address. I didn't know what the fuck was going through her head right now. I told her we were done and I meant that shit. I hadn't even been to the house, nor had I talked to her. It seemed like whenever things were going good between me and Kenzie, there's always some bullshit that got in the way.

I looked out the window to make sure Diane was leaving. Once her car was out of eyesight, I walked over to the bar and poured me a shot of Henny. I needed to have a couple drinks before going upstairs to talk to Kenzie. I already knew she was about to go in on my ass.

I was on my second shot when Tez came and sat down across from me. He grabbed the bottle and poured a drink as well. He knocked back one shot and then another one before finally opening his mouth to say something to me.

"I don't know what is going through my sister's head right now or why she's giving you another chance. To be honest, I really don't give a fuck about her reasoning. What I do care about is you hurting her in the process of whatever the hell it is you have going on right now. You need to keep your bitches in check. There is no reason why anyone should be coming where my sister and her kids lay their head at night. When a female gets comfortable enough to do that, it means they're on the crazy side and unstable. My sister doesn't need that bullshit in her life."

"I'm not on bullshit with your sister. I don't have any other bitches. I called things off with Diane a while back and I even moved out of my house to show her and your sister how serious I am. The last time Diane and I talked, I thought we had an understanding. As far as I know she's sleeping with someone else. I don't know what made her show up here because she's never did no shit like this before."

"I don't care why she did it either. All I'm saying is that you need to make sure it doesn't happen again. My sister's safety and happiness is my number one priority. It always has been and it always will be. If you don't think you can keep her happy, you need to just be there for your kids and let my sister move on with her life."

I knew Tez was only trying to look out for his sister, but I wasn't trying to hear that shit. There's absolutely nothing he could tell me right now that's going to make me change my mind about being with Kenzie, and I damn sure wasn't going to wait around for her to fall in love with someone else.

"I get where you're coming from, Tez, but you don't have anything to worry about. I have it all under control," I assured him.

"I hope you do, because you're not about to be jumping in and out of my sister's life with no consequences," Tez warned me before getting up from his seat and going downstairs to his room.

I drunk a couple more shots before finally getting up and

going upstairs to talk to Kenzie. When I got to her room, she was lying in the bed scrolling through her phone. I stripped out of my clothes then went inside the bathroom to take a quick shower. By the time I was done, Kenzie had turned the lights off and put her phone away. I knew she wasn't sleep already. She was avoiding having this conversation with me, which meant she was pissed. I didn't want either of us going to bed angry, so I turned on the light on the nightstand as I climbed into bed.

"Kenzie, we need to talk about this."

"What the fuck is there to talk about, Chase? You let that bitch find out where I live and show up at my house. Do you know how much self-control it took for me not to beat her ass for coming to my house?"

"I know, and I'm sorry. I'm not sure how she got ahold of your address. If you had beat her ass, it would have been her fault."

"No, if I had beat her ass, it would have been your fault. You've been stringing her along all this damn time. She is hurt and doesn't know what to do. I can see the shit in her eyes. You fucked her over in the process of trying to find your own happiness. I refuse to keep playing this game with you. I'm not about to be your side bitch anymore and I'm not about to do this back and forth shit with you. You're just as confused as she is when it comes to your feelings and what you want."

"Nah, I have to stop you there. I'm not confused at all and you're not my side bitch. I'm not in a relationship with her anymore. I haven't been since the twins were born. I'm not going to lie and say that I wasn't still sleeping with her sometimes, but it wasn't as often, and I never lied to her about where I was going when I came over here. When I moved out, I told her that we were done for good. I have love for Diane and I always will, but I don't love her the way I love you. I love her like I love a friend. Not enough that I would ever want to have a family with her."

"Look, this is how it's going to be. We can continue to work on getting back together but this is your last chance. You need to be open and honest with me from this day forward. If I find out you're fucking with Diane or any other bitch, we're done for good. I get to move on with my life and you're not allowed to interfere. The only thing we can do is coparent. We're getting older now and we have kids. We have to show a good example for them. I'd rather we provide two healthy households for them than one unstable household."

"I promise you don't have anything to worry about and I'm going to talk to Diane about showing up here. I'm going to make sure that she never does this shit again. I love you, Kenzie, and things are going to be different this time," I told her before leaning over and kissing her softly on the lips."

"I love you too, now you can slide over to your side of the bed because I'm going to sleep and you're not getting none tonight," she told me.

I groaned as I rolled over on my side, pulling her close to me. The funny thing was I didn't plan on trying to get none tonight. I knew she wasn't about to let me off the hook that easily. The twins would be up in a few hours and Kenzie had work in the morning, so I'd be the one to have to get up with them, so I decided to close my eyes and go to sleep as well.

I thought it would be difficult for me to be coming in doing the whole family thing, but it wasn't. I enjoyed coming in at a decent hour and getting in bed with Kenzie. I wasn't here when my kids went to bed, but I was here when they first woke up in the morning. I was working on coming in a few nights a week early enough for dinner too because I knew it was important to Kenzie.

The following morning, I woke up around five thirty to

the sound of one of my kids crying. It was only a matter of time until the other one would be up crying as well. I hurriedly climbed out of bed so they wouldn't wake Kenzie up.

I walked in the twins' nursey and made their bottles then changed their diapers. I gave them both their bottles then turned on cartoons for them. I sat in the rocking chair across from them and nodded right back off. When I woke up back up, neither of the twins were in their crib.

I got up from the chair and walked downstairs to the living room. Tez was sitting on the floor with the twins. I spoke to him then walked to the back to Kenzie's office. She was in the middle of a call when I walked in. I waited until she was finished before walking over to her.

"What time is your hair appointment?"

"It's at four. I'm going to work until three then I'm going to head out there. I know you have to work, so Tori and Tez are going to watch the twins."

"Are you sure? I can wait to go out when you get back."

"No, it's fine. Go take care of your business and I'll see you later."

I gave Kenzie a kiss on the lips then went upstairs to shower and get dressed. I was done and out of the house in an hour. I drove to my warehouse and checked on the construction. Everything was finally done, and shipments could start coming through. Having this warehouse made me feel like I was on my boss shit. I could now double up on my shipments and bring in more money than I ever had.

I stayed in the warehouse for about thirty minutes, walking around and making sure everything was complete with me and Tino's office. We also had a rec room for when there was down time. I was still debating on if I wanted to convert the warehouse into anything else. I'd hold out on that for now, though, until we got adjusted to running the warehouse accordingly.

I left the warehouse and did my weekly pickups then made my way over to the trap. I went in my office and pulled out my money counter and ledger. I put a rubber band around each stack then put the money in my safe. Once Tino finished his pickups, he'd make a bank run. By the time I finished all my work at the trap, it was six o'clock. Kenzie should almost be done with getting her hair done.

I had some down time until Tino got here and the shop was only fifteen minutes away. I hated that Kenzie still came out here to the hood to get her hair done. I tried to convince her to switch to a shop near her house or in the suburbs in general, but she wasn't having it. She'd been going to the same stylist since she was younger and she had no plans on changing that.

I pulled up to the shop and parked my car. I dapped it up with some of the guys standing outside before walking in. My eyes scanned the shop until I spotted Kenzie sitting down getting her hair done. There was some nigga all up in her face. I didn't know what he was saying, but he had her smiling and I didn't like that. I wasn't one to cause a scene in public, but I was also not going to stand around like a lame watching somebody flirt with her.

As I was walking to the back, she was digging in her purse to pay the stylist.

"How much is it?" I asked.

"Sixty-five," McKenzie replied.

I reached in my pocket and pulled out a hundred-dollar bill and handed it to the stylist. I told her to keep the change, then me and Kenzie headed out of the shop. I was about to ask her who that nigga was she was talking to when I saw a black car nearing the shop.

"Get down!" I yelled as my body shielded McKenzie's. I

could feel her body trembling up under me. I could hear people screaming and scurrying from the area. I pulled my nine out and shot back at the car as it sped away from the scene. Once the car was out of sight, I pulled Kenzie up from the ground and pulled her close to me. Tears were falling uncontrollably from her eyes.

I examined her body to make sure she wasn't hurt.

"Baby, I need you to calm down and go home. I'll be there in a minute."

"No, you need to come with me," she begged.

"I am in a—" I started but was cut off by policeman.

"Put the gun down!" the officer yelled while reaching for his own.

I did as I was told and made sure not to make any sudden moves. The officer rushed over to me and picked up the gun while the other one put me in cuffs and read me my rights. I wasn't worried about them taking me in. The gun I had was registered and I was allowed to have it. It's brand new and I didn't have any bodies on it. The most they could do was take me to the station and question me then set me a bail.

"Go home, I'll call you when I'm being released," I told McKenzie as the officer placed me in the back of his car. I just hoped Kenzie listened to me and went straight home like I told her. I didn't want to have to worry about her while I was at the station.

While I was at the station, I was questioned for almost four hours before they allowed me to call my lawyer. None of the questions they were asking had anything to do with the shooting or the gun I had. After sitting there for another three hours, Tino came and bonded me out. He drove me to my car and then I went straight to McKenzie's house. When I got there, she was sitting on the couch watching TV.

"Why are you still awake?"

"I was worried about you. Why didn't you call me?"

"I didn't want to wake you up or have you drag the twins out this late at night so I had Tino pick me up."

"So is everything alright? Do you have to go to court?"

"I just paid the fine for firing the gun and the money to be bonded out. Everything is good and we don't have anything to worry about."

"Okay, good, because your kids need you."

"Oh, only my kids need me, huh?"

"You know what I mean," she laughed.

"This is off topic, but I was talking to my mother about the holidays and told her that I was going to Miami for Christmas and New Year's to be with you, so she wanted to know if we're going to spend Thanksgiving with her and my family."

"I'm not sure. I need to talk to my mother about this because I usually spend Thanksgiving with her and my siblings because I don't spend Christmas with them."

"Okay, what if we plan a trip with both of our families for Thanksgiving? We can do a combined dinner, that way we'll be able to spend time with both of our families."

"Alright, I'll look up some places and let you know what I find out."

McKenzie and I sat up and talked for about an hour before we both finally laid down and fell asleep. I prayed this would be the one night the twins would sleep longer, because neither of us had had any sleep.

CHAPTER SEVEN

BLAZE

Over the past seven weeks, I've been pushing my body to its limit. I've been going through therapy working on my lower and upper body strength. My cast came off last week and I can feel the sensation in my legs and arms again. You don't know how relieved I was when I found out I wasn't paralyzed and none of the nerve damage was permanent. I don't know how I would have survived being in a wheelchair because I'm too damn independent for that shit.

I still have a slight limp right now, but my physical therapist said that should be going away the more I put pressure on my legs. She tried to get me to walk with a cane but I'm too much of G for that.

All of my scars are completely healed and it feels good to move my neck without worrying about if I'm about to bust a stitch or not. For the first couple of weeks after the shooting, I ended up having to wear a neck brace because I wouldn't keep still. The shit was awkward as hell to me.

I'm glad Rafael didn't do a bubble-gum job with my

stitches. The scars I have are barely visible. When I look at them, though, it reminds me of how close I was to losing my life. I don't know if the lifestyle I'm living is worth it anymore. Don't get me wrong now, I don't have no bitch in my blood. My thought process has to do with my kids and the women in my life, such as my baby mamas, family, and Kenzie. Yeah, I still factor Kenzie in my life because I haven't given up on her yet. Time just still isn't quite on our side yet, but it will be soon.

I'm really out here doing this shit just because. I have more than enough money to retire from the drug game and still maintain the lifestyle that I live comfortably and be able to pass down generational wealth. It's not like I'll be broke or a bum ass nigga. I still have all my legal businesses that bring in hella revenue.

Part of me hasn't slowed down with this shit yet because I don't want to disappoint my brother. We took over this shit to keep my pops's legacy going. It's easier to say you're going to quit the game than actually quitting. There's so many families that depend on me. I can't let my people down like that in the spur of the moment. If I ever leave, I have to give them a notice, but I know if I want to get married and have more kids, I'm not going to be able to balance it all at once.

I looked over at the clock and saw that it was almost 11:30. I've been lying here looking at the ceiling for almost an hour, thinking. I have so much shit I need to do but in order for me to do it, I have to be at my best. I'm about ready to stop taking these meds and get back to my regular life. I'm not used to sleeping in and laying down not doing anything. Everyone wants me to take it easy, but it's not that simple for me. I need to be able to get up and make moves on my own so I can show my brother I'm strong enough to travel.

I miss the hell out of Kenzie, the twins, and my son. I haven't seen him in person since the day Tamika came out here when I woke up after my accident. I wanted him to stay with me but he has school and she has work, a husband, and another child at home. I talk to him on FaceTime every day, but it's not the same. Thanksgiving is in a couple weeks and he'll be on break for a few days, so Josh is going to bring him down here with him since he, Nita, and the kids are spending the holiday with me.

I'm glad about that because it's been a minute since I was able to hang out with Josh. During the time I was away, I only saw Josh if I was in Chicago handling business. I was never there for more than two days at a time.

I climbed out of bed and threw on a pair of basketball shorts, a wife beater, and a pair of white Ones. I walked out of the room and downstairs to the kitchen where Kim, Tasia, and Kayla were sitting down eating. I picked my daughter up and sat her on my lap.

"Are you hungry? Your plate is in the microwave. I can warm it up for you," Tasia offered.

"I'll get it after my therapy session," I replied.

"I don't know why you're still going through therapy when Tasia and I have been able to help you just as much as she has," Kim said.

"I just got up, Kim, don't start this. It was an eight-week therapy session program so I'm going to finish my eight weeks," I told her.

"Yeah, I bet, so you can have an excuse for little miss Akina to come over here half naked," she said before walking out of the room.

Tasia laughed at her, but all I could do was shake my head at her antics. I'll give her some D later and she'll be okay.

My life is like a hood movie right now. I still can't believe I'm living it. If you would have told me that Kim, Tasia, and I would be able to live under the same roof drama free, I would have called you crazy. The first week after I got shot it was tension having both of them under the same roof because they both were fighting for attention that I couldn't give neither of them because I was laid up in bed, so the shit was stupid as hell. I got tired of the back and forth, so I sat them both down and had a talk with them. I reminded them that I wasn't in a relationship with either of them so I was free to do whatever I wanted.

I informed them that I needed them both there for different reasons and they needed to find a way to get along. Tasia had to be here for safety purposes. I wasn't letting her go back to Chicago until I go back because she needs a new house and this time, I'm picking it for her. Kim was still here because she knew too much of what went down and there was still a job I needed her to do. I told them if it would make them more comfortable, I won't touch either of them while we're under the same roof. At the time they were fine with that because sex wasn't on my mind and I could barely move. That changed, though, once I started physical therapy and moving around.

I guess being in the house with someone changes your perspective of them. Kim and Tasia started getting close over time because if they weren't helping me eat, change clothes, or exercise, all they had was each other's company because my brother's wife, Myra, was busy most of the time with the kids or helping my brother with business. She didn't touch the drugs but she did do accountant work and count the money for him.

One night, Tasia and Kim came in my bedroom and told me that they came to an agreement. They both wanted me and since we're all stuck in the house together, we should all be together and there will be no jealousy involved. I called bull-shit until they started making out and eating each other's pussy in front of me, causing my dick to rock up. That was the first time in three weeks that I had an erection. I swear to God I thought my shit was broke and I was going to need the tiny blue pills. I could tell that wasn't the first time they did that with each other, but I'm guessing they needed some dick added to the equation and I was fair game.

Ever since that day, we were all on one accord. We shared a bed together and most of the time we had threesomes and some of the time, I was fucking whichever one of them came to me for dick when the other one wasn't around.

Now hold on, before you bash me, because this was never my plan. I never intended on fucking with Tasia or Kim again after my accident. I was going to have a clean slate and once my therapy was up, I was going to go home to Kenzie.

Kenzie was treating me like I was some kind of lame and I didn't know any other way to deal with how I was feeling except for me to do me, because clearly that's what she was doing. I wasn't used to females getting down on me like this. Females begged me to give them the time of day. They yearned for my attention, not the other way around. Dealing with a female like Kenzie will humble the shit out of you. That's why most street niggas go after bitches that don't have shit going for themselves, because they be wanting someone to show them that they're needed to help boost their ego. We be needing someone to worship the ground we walk on and make us feel like a god.

That's one of the reasons why I'm tied up with Kim and Tasia right now. What man don't want two bad bitches at his beck and call. Ready to feed and fuck him until he passes out. It's fun for now but it does get old sometimes, and that's why I could never settle down with either one of them. I'll never be able to take them seriously, and that's why I know for this next level and journey I'm going to take, Kenzie needs to be there. She calls me out on my shit and what I say don't always go.

That's why my situation is conflicting, and I haven't given up on her.

Since Kenzie has me blocked, I was sending messages through Lauren for her but she was never sending any back. I don't know if she forgot that I was still friends with her on social media or she just didn't care, but there was pictures of her, Chase, and the twins up and down her page. They looked like one big happy family. That shit pissed me off because I knew there was a chance that she'd start back fucking with him again, but I didn't expect her to say fuck me and start a relationship with the nigga in the process. Here I was shot multiple times, going through recovery, and not one time did she bother to reach out to me again to see how I was doing. I know I was wrong for telling her not to come see me, but if I knew she was going to take it as never seeing me again, I wouldn't have said shit and let her ass come here and dealt with the consequences then.

I played with my daughter for a few minutes then headed downstairs to the gym because Akina should be here soon. I sat on one of the benches and like clockwork, she came strolling in the gym with a tiny pair of biker shorts and a sports bra. I know she does it to get under Kim's skin because when she first started coming, she was wearing a t-shirt and leggings, until one day Kim told her that she needed to dress more appropriate and that I'd never give her the time of day. I checked Kim about that, but Akina chose to kill her with kindness.

"Hey handsome, you're ready to get sweaty?" Akina flirted.

"You already know what time it is. I'm ready when you are."

"Now don't say that, because I like to read in between the lines and you know I been ready for you," she said as she licked her lips, causing my dick to jump.

"Girl, you better stop playing with me before I fuck your life up. You not ready for a man like me. Now come and let's get this session over," I told her.

She looked like she wanted to say something else but instead, she squatted in front of me and lifted my legs so we could work on my stretches.

Akina is as bad as a two-year-old child. She's chocolate with clear skin and a toned body. I'm talking about you can't find an ounce of fat or a stretch mark on her, she has washboard abs, perky breasts with long legs, and a nice ass that fits her physique. I guess it's the perks of being a physical therapist.

Akina's never hidden the fact that she wants to fuck. If I didn't have to finish therapy sessions with her, I would have been bent her over one of these benches and gave her the work, not caring who else was in the house, but I don't mix business with pleasure. Besides, I have enough woman problems as it is. On our last day of therapy, I'll probably give her what she wants to get it out of my system because after that, I'm done with all this shit.

Playtime will be officially over and I'll be back to business. I'm cutting Kim, Tasia, and any other woman that's had my attention before off for good. The days of Kenzie and I dealing with other people will be a distance memory. I'm devoting all of my focus on her only. I already have it planned out. I'm just counting down to Lauren's wedding where she won't be able to avoid me.

I don't know if it was because I was caught up in my thoughts or if Akina's touch was so soft that I didn't realize how far her hand had gone up my leg until I felt her massaging my dick. I could have stopped her right then and there, but I was curious to see how far she was actually going to go and if I'm being honest, the shit was feeling good as hell.

I looked down and locked eyes with Akina. When she realized I wasn't going to stop her, she pulled my dick completely out of my shorts and began stroking it. Since she wanted to take it there with me, I grabbed her jaw and pushed my dick in her mouth then started moving her head up and down at a slow pace. I closed my eyes and leaned my back against the wall when she started twirling her tongue around it. I grabbed her ponytail and started making her deepthroat me, and I was surprised when she didn't gag. She was sucking my dick like a champ.

"Shit, do yo' thing, ma," I groaned, letting her head go. She continued at the same pace, making sure to move her tongue side to side. I was weak in the knees and ready to bust already. She lifted her head up some, leaving some of my dick in her mouth, and she started sucking and slurping before pushing me back in her mouth until the point that I could feel the back of her throat.

"I'm about to nut," I warned her. She slid me out of her mouth, and I thought she was done until she started twirling her tongue on the tip. Once she started sucking my mushroom again, it was over with. I busted in her mouth, and she made sure to swallow every drop.

"Tasty, just as I thought," Akina said as she wiped my nut off the side of her mouth. She stuck my dick back in my shorts and stood from the floor. I could tell she was wet from sucking my dick because I could see the wet spot in between her legs.

"Pull your shorts down then bend over and touch your toes," I ordered.

She did as she was told, and her pussy was glistening, just as I thought. If I had a condom, I would have fucked her, but I didn't have one so I did the alternative. I spit on the tip of my fingers then rubbed her clit, causing her to instantly squirm.

All it took was a good three minutes of playing in her pussy and she was gushing like a broken faucet.

I got up from my seat and walked over to the sink and wet one of the towels then handed it to her so she could clean herself.

"When are you going to let me ride your dick like I just rode your fingers? I won't tell you girlfriends, I know how to keep a secret."

"It's not about them and they're not my girlfriends. I just don't want to complicate things between us since we still have two weeks of therapy to go. Don't worry, though, I gotcha," I assured her.

Our hour was up, so my session was done for the day. I walked Akina out then I went to the kitchen to eat my food. So much for waiting until my therapy was over to fuck her. I was definitely going to hit when she came back in two days.

CHAPTER EIGHT
MCKENZIE

It's been two months since I last spoke to Malakai. It's not because he hasn't contacted me, but it's because I have him on my block list. That still doesn't stop him from sending gifts to me and the kids. He even relays messages through Lauren sometimes, but I never tell her to tell him anything back. I know I might be being petty, but I don't care.

Chase and I are officially back together. I guess you can even say he lives with me. We never discussed him moving in with me. He just continued to come to my house every night and I never stopped him. Things have been great between us though. We have date night every Friday, and Saturdays are dedicated to our kids. Sometimes we stay in all day with them and if the weather permits, we take them out. It feels good to have my personal little family.

Chase makes sure to be home for dinner at least twice a week and the days that he's not he's home by midnight. It's like he's the Chase I fell in love with three years ago. I tried my best to keep my guard up, but he's slowly breaking it down again. I know I might be settling for Chase, but if Malakai really wanted to be with me, he would have came back to Chicago and proved it to me already. I know for a fact he's done with his physical therapy and he's up walking around because Lauren told me that as well. That means he's just in LA living his best life with Kim and Tasia. I refuse to sit here and look dumb and desperate waiting on his ass. I'm not going to lie and say I don't love him anymore but in this case, love isn't enough.

Me and Chase's families agreed on combining Thanksgiving together, so we decided on going to Gatlinburg, Tennessee. We rented a cabin that sleeps forty-six people with 8.5 bathrooms. There's a movie theater, hot tub, indoor swimming pool plus a rec room with a pool table and other game equipment. We were going to do two separate cabins that held twenty-two people apiece, but then there wouldn't be enough table space for everyone to sit down for dinner. Chase also thought it was a good idea for our families to get to know each other, but I didn't really care about that part. He was footing the bill for this trip, though, so I let him have his way.

Thanksgiving is tomorrow, and we'll be staying here until Saturday, so I pray we can survive the next few days here without anyone killing each other. Since Chase and I are hosting this thing, he, Tori, and I came in yesterday to make sure everything was straight with the house to help accommodate all these motherfuckers.

My father, Lauren, Martez, and McKenna wanted to spend more time with us and also help me get everything together, so they came in last night. The rest of my family and Chase's will be here sometime today and tomorrow. If my father and brother would have said they couldn't make it out here, I would have said fuck this whole idea. I was going to need them, Lauren, and a lot of alcohol to help get me through this shit because Ricky, Juliet, and Aunt Cathy are going to be here, and I can't stand none of their asses. Some of Aniya and Tyrese's family are even going to be here. This is going to be one big, blended family event that can make or break some relationships.

I put on my sandals to go with the brown sundress I was wearing then headed down the stairs. I kissed my kids on the forehead then grabbed my keys to the Escalade we rented. Tori, Lauren, and I left the house to go grocery shopping. It took about twenty minutes for us to get there. I drove around the parking lot until I found a spot not too far from the entrance. We each grabbed a grocery cart because we have a lot of shit to get. We not only have to get the ingredients for Thanksgiving dinner, but we also need to grab groceries for the next couple of days. Dinner was at each person's disposal, but I also wanted to have food in the house in case people didn't want to eat out every day.

We walked around the grocery store for almost an hour sticking stuff in our carts. By the time we were done, we had three carts piled up to the rim.

"Damn, can I come to dinner with y'all?" this fine ass light-skin brother asked us.

"I don't think our men will approve," I answered.

"Shit, I can say I'm your long-lost cousin," he joked.

"Nah, we're good," Lauren added.

I laughed at Lauren's no-nonsense tone as we walked to the checkout line, leaving him standing there alone. The lines were moving fast until we made it to the front of the line. The cashier looked at us and huffed as we started putting our things on the conveyor belt. The people standing behind us were mumbling under their voices as well, but I ignored them.

"Is all of this together?" the cashier asked with a slight attitude.

"Yup, and make sure to double our bags," I told her with a smile.

"Damn, this line is moving slow as hell. They have to feed an army or some shit," one of the customers behind us said.

"Uhm, you do know you can take your ass to another line if this one moving too slow for you. You saw these carts when your ass got in line," I pointed out.

The lady looked like she wanted to say something, but she changed her mind when Tori gave her a look daring her to jump hard with me.

"Your total is $1,435.25. Will you be paying with link?" the cashier said loudly.

That was it, I had enough of her attitude.

"No, bitch, I'm paying with debit, and if your ass didn't want to come to work and do your job you should have stayed your ass at home," I snapped before swiping my debit card. I didn't have anything against people that got link. Hell, my mother used to get link at one point. My issue was that people automatically thought you were using link since you were Black with a cart full of groceries.

We pushed our carts outside and packed the car up. I was glad we had the truck, or all of our groceries wouldn't have fit. I tossed the keys to Lauren and let her drive. We put away all of the groceries then headed back to the cabin. The guys came out and got the groceries. We started putting them away as they brought them in. By the time we were done, we ordered pizzas, wings, and pasta for dinner because we didn't have time to cook dinner plus prep for Thanksgiving. Not to mention there was no telling who all would be making it in tonight, so we wanted to have food for them.

The guys sat around and watched TV while Tori, Lauren, and I started on the dishes we were making for tomorrow. I'm making the mac and cheese, Lauren is making cherry pies, and

Tori is making the spaghetti. My father and Tez will be deep frying turkeys tomorrow. The rest of the food will be cooked by my mother, Juliet, and some of our aunts. There was no way I was doing all this cooking on my own.

An hour later, the food was delivered and Tez set it all up. A couple minutes after that, the doorbell went off and it was my siblings, Quan, Ricky, and my mother. I spoke to them then got back to what I was doing. When I was done prepping the food I wrapped it in foil and put it in the refrigerator. I'll put it in the oven tomorrow before dinner. It was already eight so Lauren and I got the twins and McKenna ready for bed. My father had a king bed in his room to himself, so he volunteered to have his grandkids sleep with him. I was fine with that because it would give Chase and I some time alone. If my father didn't get the kids, then they would be sleeping in our room with us.

I went back downstairs and made my plate. The guys were in a heated game of spades, and I wanted no parts of that, so I grabbed a bottle of Patrón then sat down on the couch with it.

Tori, Lauren, and I were sitting on the couch chilling when Aniyah wabbled over to us. She was seven months pregnant with a little boy. I can't wait to meet and spoil my nephew. Aniyah and I are back on good terms and our relationship is how it used to be when we were younger. I'm happy about that because I want our kids to have a close relationship with each other.

We sat around and talked until the guys finally finished playing cards. After that, Chase and I went upstairs to our bedroom. We took a hot shower and washed each other's bodies. Once we were done, we got out and moisturized our bodies before climbing into bed. Chase wasted no time crashing his lips into mine. He broke the kiss and put one of my nipples into his mouth, causing me to moan out loud. His hand traveled down my body and made its way in between my leg.

He teased my clit and by now, I was dripping wet. He slowly pushed a finger in and out of me.

I arched my back and rocked back and forth on his fingers. I was on the brink of cumming when he stopped. I was about to go off on his ass until he trailed kisses down my body and his lips latched onto my throbbing clit. I held onto the back of his head and my legs started to shake. He continued to suck and slurp on my clit until I was cumming all over his face. I tried to push his head off, but he slapped my hand away. He continued devouring me until I was cumming again.

Chase came up for air and crashed his lips into mine, allowing me to taste my own juices as he slowly pushed himself inside of me, causing both us to moan out loud.

"Damn, baby, your shit wet as hell," he moaned into my ear as he bit down on it, causing my pussy to erupt instantly.

He started off slow then started pounding in and out of me. Lifting my leg into the crook of his arm so he can get a better angle of my spot.

"Oh my god, Chase, you're about to make me cum again," I called out.

"Let that shit out, baby!" Chase boasted as he hit my spot every time.

"Arggghh," I cried as I started squirting everywhere.

Chase flipped me over and plunged right back in my pussy from the back. I arched my back and Chase pushed my head into the pillow so the whole house couldn't hear what we were doing. By that time, I was a mess and had lost count of how many times I came before Chase finally came.

Chase laid down on his back and he was still hard, so I climbed on top of him and started riding like my life depended on it.

"Fuck, slow down, Kenzie, you're going to make me nut quick," Chase warned me.

"I'm almost there too, don't stop," I demanded.

Chase never could handle when I rode his dick. I had already busted multiple times so I didn't care if he came or not. He held my waist with one hand and rubbed my clit with the other one, driving me crazy. I bit down on my lip so I wouldn't yell out in pleasure.

"I'm about to nut," Chase grunted.

"Hold on, I'm right there with you," I cried out.

I rolled off of Chase and laid down on the bed, trying to catch my breath. We let a few minutes pass before I got out of bed to take a shower because there was cum dripping down my legs. Chase got up and joined me, so we washed each other up again before laying down in bed. Normally we would watch a movie until we fell asleep, but there was no need tonight because both of us were tired.

CHAPTER NINE
CHASE

The next day I woke up around 10 o'clock and Kenzie was still knocked out sleep. I smiled at how beautiful she looked while sleeping. She didn't tie her hair up last night so it was sprawled all over her head. I leaned over and kissed her on the forehead then climbed out of bed. I put on a pair of boxers, basketball shorts, and a t-shirt before heading down the stairs. My mom, Aunt Jillian, Celeste, Cathy, and some other lady who I don't know were in the kitchen cooking for the dinner. They had the house smelling good as hell. I couldn't wait to eat dinner.

I spoke to everyone then hugged my mother and aunt.

"When did y'all get here?" I asked my mother.

"We made it around two this morning. Your brother, Jennifer, and the kids are upstairs still in bed. I took a nap for a couple hours then came down and started getting dinner together."

"Okay, do you all need help with anything?"

"No, we're good, but everyone is still sleeping and the stove is being occupied, so y'all will have to figure out what to do about food until dinner time."

"Kenzie bought fruit, cereal, and a bunch of other breakfast stuff yesterday. It's in the other refrigerator, so we'll be good."

"That's good, where is she now? How y'all hosting Thanksgiving but she's still asleep?"

"It's too early for your foolishness, Juliet. Let that girl sleep. There's no room for her to put anything else in that oven right now," Aunt Jillian said to my mother.

I was glad my aunt spoke up because I didn't feel like dealing with my mother's bullshit.

I left the kitchen area and sat down on the couch. A few minutes later, Lauren came down with both of the twins.

"They're just waking up?" I asked.

"Of course not, they woke up at six and Victor changed their diapers and fed them. He stayed up with them until about an hour ago, then he went outside with Tez to start on the turkeys. Since I was up, I went in the room and laid down with them until Kenna woke up. Is Kenzie still asleep? I was going to get them dressed for her."

"Yeah, she is, but you can give them to me. I'll get them dressed in a little while."

"That's okay, I want to keep them. I'm trying to convince Kenzie to let the kids go back with us since she'll be out there in a couple weeks anyway, but she hasn't given me an answer yet."

"She talked to me about that and I told her I was fine with whatever she decided. I know she could use the break but at the same time, she'll miss them and end up flying out to Miami a couple days after y'all gone."

"You know I'm fine with that because I miss her, and she can come down early to finish helping me get everything together for my bachelorette party and wedding."

"You already taking her away from me for two weeks as it is."

Lauren's bachelorette party is the third Saturday in December, and the wedding is the following weekend on Christmas Eve. Kenzie is flying in the Monday before the party, and I'll be flying in the day before the wedding and staying until New Year's.

"I know, but that's my sissy pooh," Lauren laughed.

I took the twins from Lauren and placed them in their play pen. I was about to go find something to eat when the sound of the doorbell went off. I walked over and opened the door without saying who is it. I instantly regretted opening the door.

"What the hell are y'all doing here?" I asked, looking between Diane and Shavon.

"Your mother didn't tell you that we were coming?" Diane inquired.

"Ma, what the hell is this? Why would you invite her here?" I asked as calmly as possible, but my blood was boiling on the inside.

"Boy, move out the way and let that girl in. We always spend Thanksgiving together as a family, so where was she supposed to go?"

"This some bullshit and you know it," I replied.

"I'm sorry, Chase, your mother told me that she talked to you about this and you said you were fine with this," Diane added.

"You should have called me first. You know damn well I would have told your ass not to come all the way out here. You can come in, but stay away from me," I told her as I stepped to the side."

"You have to got be fucking kidding me. You invited that bitch and your ex here?" Kenzie screeched behind me.

"Baby, of course not. I wouldn't do no shit like this. My mother invited Diane and Shavon came with her. I only let them in because they made this long drive out here."

Instead of responding to me, Kenzie turned around and stormed back up the stairs. I was about to chase after her, but Lauren stopped me.

"You need to deal with this shit down here and I'll go up there and talk to Kenzie."

"Juliet, you're too damn old for all this dumb shit you're doing. That boy has a family with someone else and you're still trying to force that damn girl on him. Don't you realize if you keep this shit up, you're going to lose your son? Because you know he's not going to pick you over his kids," my aunt told my mother.

"Shut up and mind your own business. That is my son and I know what's good for him. Why should that homewrecking bitch get to have everything that she wants?" my mother replied.

"Hold on now, I've kept quiet because I don't get involved in my daughter's business, but I'm not going to stand here and listen to you disrespect her. Your son was the one chasing after my daughter, not the other way around, so your anger is misdirected in the wrong direction."

I could feel the tension in the house and at the rate it was going, we weren't going to make it to dinner.

"Ma, Celeste and Aunt Jillian are right. I'm getting tired of this shit and it ends now. This shit is getting played out now. You knew I was messing with Kenzie from the beginning. She's the mother of my kids and you need to respect her."

"I don't need to respect nobody that I don't like," my mother spat.

"You don't have a reason not to like her. I was the one that cheated and got Kenzie pregnant. I was the one not man enough to let Diane know that I didn't want or love her anymore. You're acting like I cheated and broke your heart or some shit," I bellowed.

I know I was wrong for talking to my mother like this, but I had enough for real. This song and dance was getting old. My kids were damn near one already. I went and talked to Diane a couple days after she came to Kenzie's house, and I apologized for leading her on, but I told her we could never be together again. Even if I wasn't with Kenzie, I still wouldn't get back in a relationship with Diane and she claimed she understood. However, her showing up here now had me rethinking whether she understood where I was coming from or not.

"Boy, who the hell do you think you talking to like that? I will knock your ass upside your head with one of these frying pans. Now shut your ass up and go show them to a room."

"I'm not showing them to shit. You invited them so you show them to a room," I told her before going upstairs to check on Kenzie.

I walked in the room and Kenzie was pacing the floor while Lauren was sitting on the bed trying to calm her down. As soon as Kenzie saw me, she grabbed the brush from the nightstand and threw it, barely missing my head.

"What the fuck are you doing up here? I know you didn't leave my kids downstairs with them!" Kenzie yelled.

"I came up here to check on you. The kids are in their play pen. Nobody is going to do anything to them," I assured her.

"I'm not trying to hear that shit. Go get my kids, Chase. This is some straight bullshit."

"I'll go downstairs with them so you two can talk," Lauren volunteered.

"Baby, I need you to calm down. I swear I didn't know they were going to be here. I already told them to make sure they stay away from us while they're here."

"So we're actually about to share a house with your ex and my bitch of a stepsister? You better be ready to bail me out of jail, because I already know I'm going to have to beat somebody's ass before this trip is over."

"You're not going to have to fight anyone, and you don't have anything to worry about. You're the one that I'm with. I don't want Diane, so you don't have to worry about that."

"I'm not worried about that. I'm worried about somebody saying some slick shit out of their mouth that's going to piss me off. We both already know Diane is a puppet with Shavon's hand up her back."

"Look, it's the holidays, so let's just get through tonight. If the dinner doesn't go well, we can get up and leave in the morning. I promise I won't go anywhere with Diane alone. I know you're not worried about me cheating with her, but I don't want you to have a reason to question me about her."

"Okay, but you better make sure they both stay away from me, because there's no way in hell Diane could have thought this was a good idea for her to come here. She knew I was going to be here, so I'm not sure what her angle is but it can't be good."

"I agree with you there, but as long as she stay away from us I don't care what angle she is playing. I also checked my mother for this bullshit she pulled."

"Good, that'll save me a trip from having to do it, because her old ass has run out of chances with me. Your mother better stay the hell away from me too," McKenzie said seriously.

Normally, I wouldn't let anyone make a threat toward my mother, but I know Kenzie is upset and she has every right to be. This was the most outrageous shit my mother has ever done. I have no idea what is going through her head or what she expected the outcome of this will be.

"Do you want to go out to eat or explore the area so you can calm down?"

"Nope, because unfortunately, I have to go put the macaroni in the oven and start setting the tables for dinner. Dinner is at four, so I hope everyone else gets here on time."

"I'm sure they will. If not, that's on them. They knew about this trip two months ago."

"Okay, I hope so, because I'm ready for this dinner to be over already and it hasn't even started yet," Kenzie said before walking past me and out of the door.

I followed behind her because I didn't want to take any chances of anything jumping off. I was relieved to see Tori and Charmaine downstairs. I know they can keep Kenzie level headed.

I went outside with Victor and Tez to help them out. It was best that I stay out of the way until it was time for dinner.

"Yo, what's your mother's problem?" Tez asked me.

"Man, I don't know. I thought she was over me being with Diane. She accepted the kids and she kept her cool around Kenzie."

"I don't care about her keeping her cool around Kenzie. This shit is foul that she just pulled. You better make sure this night goes smooth and no shit jumps off between my sister and them girls."

"Like I told McKenzie, I have this under control. Diane knows she better stay in her place."

"For her sake and yours, I hope you're right," Tez replied as he picked up the turkey and took it in the house, leaving me standing outside alone looking stupid.

"Yo, you're good, bro?" Tino asked behind me.

"Hell no, why didn't you tell me they were coming here?"

"Come on now, you know I didn't know this or I would have made Mama tell her not come. I'm going to talk to Ma about this later, though, because she doesn't realize that giving Diane hopes of being with you is only hurting her even more in the process."

"I just need Mama to stay out of my business and allow me to live my life the way I want with the person I want."

"At this point, you have to put your foot down with Diane. Tell her it's time for her to find a place and get out of your house. It's time for you to break all ties with her and if she wants to still be in contact with Ma, then that has nothing to do with you."

I listened to everything Tino was saying and he was right. It's time for me to stop being nice to Diane and considering her feelings. While I'm considering her feelings, I'm not thinking about the woman I'm with feelings. I should never have put Kenzie in an uncomfortable position like this. If I kept this shit up, Kenzie was going to leave my ass, and Diane or my mama were not worth it.

CHAPTER TEN
MCKENZIE

In spite of Diane and Shavon showing up yesterday for Thanksgiving, I was back in a good mood. I couldn't allow them to knock me off my square or give them the satisfaction of thinking they fazed me. I thought were going to have a dinner from hell, but it went off without a hitch. Everyone respected each other for the sake of the holiday. We ate, talked, and tried to get to know each other better. I was glad about that because in some way or another, we were all family and tied to each other, whether it was by blood or through relationships.

Once dinner was over, some people played games while other ones watched movies or went outside to enjoy the weather. Of course, I stayed in because I love playing family games. It was something I always did at my mother's house when I was younger and when I was with my dad's family in Miami. Family has always been the most important thing to me. That's why I valued their opinion so much and I was big on loyalty.

Diane kept her word and stayed away from Chase and I for

the most part. I would catch her staring a little too hard if he hugged or kissed me. He made sure to make me feel secure and show that I didn't have anything to worry about. He was just as affectionate with me here in front of everyone as he is when we're at home alone.

Juliet, of course, had to prove a point and let it be known that she was in the room but eventually, everyone started ignoring her, including her own family. For her to have a job, she hit the bottle a lot. I would hate to ever be a patient of hers. I really think Chase and Tino should get her some help, but it's not my place to tell them. In the meantime, she will never have my kids alone until they know how to talk and dial my number. She won't go on an alcohol binge and leave mine unattended. No ma'am, no sir, because that will be the day I forget that she's Chase's mother.

Shavon and Quan were a little too friendly for me in Aniyah's face. I was just waiting on Aniyah to say something so I can jump in and handle her light weight, but she remained quiet the whole time. Couldn't be me, I don't give a fuck if I forgave either of their asses, you're not going to be having an intimate conversation with the bitch I caught you cheating with. I don't give a fuck how much I claim to trust their asses.

That's why I get where Diane was coming from to an extent. I never expected her to be my friend because I never had intentions on being hers. I was the one that her man cheated on her with for over a year and got pregnant. Even when I found out he was with her first, that didn't stop me from letting him fuck. I knew I was in the wrong, but I didn't care because my feelings were involved.

It's now Friday afternoon and I just woke up from a nap. Everyone is up and doing their own thing. Lauren and Tez took the twins with them outside. I'm not exactly sure where they went, but I know my kids are in good hands with them. I wanted to soak in the Jacuzzi, so I put on my brown two-piece swimsuit along with a wrap and a pair of slides. I brushed my hair up into a high bun because I didn't feel like washing or straightening it again if it got wet and curly.

I walked past my father's room and heard the TV on, so I decided to go in and talk to him for a little while first since we haven't talked much since he's been out here. I turned the knob and regretted not knocking first.

"What the hell, why didn't y'all lock the door?" I screeched as I hurriedly closed the door. I was going to be scarred for life after seeing my parents in bed together. I didn't even know they still talked to each other now that I'm grown let alone had sex. My mother didn't need to be with Ricky or my father. I loved my father to death, but he was not a man to have a relationship with because he didn't show love and he was married as well.

I stayed outside the door for almost ten minutes until my father finally opened the door. I couldn't believe their asses actually made me wait for them to finish.

"McKenzie, where are your manners? I know I taught you to knock on doors before you open them," my father chastised me with his thick accent.

"Lo siento, Papa, but I didn't expect to walk in on you doing that. I was just coming to talk to you."

"What, you think you're the only one out here being grown now? I'm not too old to have sex," he said, making my skin crawl.

"Ew, gross, I don't want to hear about that, Papa."

"Welcome to my world. Do you think I wanted to know that my princesa was having sex?"

"Okay, I guess you have a point there, but still. How long has this been going on between you two?"

"Off and on since you were little. Whenever your father

came to get you, I'd come to his hotel when you and Tez were asleep and be out before you two woke up. We stopped for a while but then started up again when you had your car accident. While I was there helping you, I was spending time with your father at night," my mother admitted.

I don't know how I didn't see the signs or missed this shit. They never gave any indication that they were even still interested in each other. I can't wait until Tez gets back to find out if he knows about this.

"So what is this, do you two plan on trying to get together or are y'all just screwing?" I asked, confused. It's baffling that I'm even having this conversation with my parents.

"It's not as simple as that, McKenzie, and you know it. Your mother is married, and I'm semi-married. We just go with the flow of things when we see each other. That's how it's always been with us and that's how it always will be."

"I guess, you two are grown and it's your life. Do whatever floats your boat," I told them before walking out of the room. I hope my mother knew what she was doing sleeping with my father behind Ricky's back. Most of all, I hope her feelings aren't involved with my father or she will be the one that ends up hurt in the end.

There was a tradition in my father's family that in order to take over the family business you have to be twenty-five and married. Two months away from my father's twenty-fifth birthday, he was a single father to a two-year-old son and nowhere near close to marrying anyone. My grandfather introduced him to his business partner's daughter, Isabella. They suggested him and Isabella get married so their companies could merge.

My father had no intentions on settling down, but he agreed to it for the money. Ever since then, their marriage has been unconventional, and my father can pretty much do whatever he wants except bring women into their homes and another child. Isabella accepted me when my father told her about me because she couldn't have kids, but she told him that he better not allow it to happen again. My father didn't mind because he had his son and daughter. He didn't want any more kids after us anyway.

I walked downstairs and to the pool area. It looked like that's where mostly everyone chose to hang out. I looked around and didn't see Chase, so I walked to the other side where the Jacuzzi was. I pushed the door halfway open and stopped in my tracks when I heard Chase talking to Shavon.

"Move before I beat your ass again. I got out of the pool because of you, so I don't know why the fuck you followed me in here. You trying get both our asses whooped by Kenzie."

"Kenzie not gone do shit, it's not my fault your bitch insecure and don't want you around us. I'm just trying to find out when you gone let me ride that dick again."

"Bitch, shut up, I told you to stay the fuck away from me that night and I meant it. That was a mistake and you know it."

"Well, it's a mistake I'm willing to let happen again."

"I don't give a fuck—" Chase started but stopped when I pushed the door all the way open and walked in. He jumped out of the Jacuzzi and made his way toward me.

I had heard enough, and I couldn't believe my ears. This nigga fucked this dusty ass bitch too.

"Oh no, don't stop on my accord. Gone ahead and finish y'all conversation," I insisted.

"How much did you hear? I can explain everything."

"Explain what? How your dog ass was fucking my stepsister behind my back? That's fucking low, even for you."

"I swear to God it's not like that, Kenzie."

"You don't have to lie or sugar coat shit for that bitch. Tell her how we fucked when you came home one night after leaving hers. I'm guessing you didn't fuck him good enough that night because he was all up in this pussy enjoying every bit of it," she teased.

My anger got the best of me and the next thing I knew, I swung and punched Chase in his eye. His reflexes must've kicked in, because he reached out and slapped the shit out of me and before I knew it, I started throwing blows all over his face and chest. I didn't give a fuck where I hit him at, but I made sure every hit landed. Instead of fighting back, he gripped me up by neck, but that didn't stop me from getting one more good lick in his mouth.

"Let me the fuck go," I demanded.

"You out your rabbit ass mind. Keep your motherfucking hands to yourself," he ordered before releasing me.

I instantly started going right back off on his trifling ass. I was so caught up with arguing with Chase that I didn't notice Shavon's dog-face ass run up on me. She grabbed me by the back of my hair and pulled me backward. The bitch had really fucked up then because I wasn't even going to touch her. This one was all on Chase because he knew better and yet again, I was never one to fight over a nigga, but I definitely wasn't about to let a bitch run up on me.

"Let her fucking hair go!" Chase yelled as he pushed Shavon up off of me.

"Bitch, you want to run up on me? I see you ain't learn your lesson from the last ass whooping I gave you!" I shouted as I ran up on her, punching her in her face. I could feel my knuckles bruising as I went blow for blow. Shavon tried to dodge my punches, but I was too fast for her. Blood was leaking from her nose and mouth. All she could was take the punches and scratch me. She got a few good licks off on me too, but they didn't faze me. This ass whooping was well deserved for what she did to my sister. You won't make me believe that she and Quan still not fucking behind Aniyah's back.

"Aye, break that shit up," Ricky ordered as he roughly grabbed me off Shavon, and that was the wrong move for him to make because he started getting the blows that were meant for his daughter. By this time, everyone was coming to see what the commotion was, and I was like a wild beast on a mission. It took Chase to pull me up off his ass.

I didn't know Tez was back until he came running over to where I was.

"Yo, didn't I warn you what would happen if you fucked with my sister again?" Tez asked as he punched Ricky in the jaw so hard his ass went flying into the Jacuzzi.

"That's enough, Kenz, you proved your point," Chase whispered in my ear, but I wasn't trying to hear nothing he was saying. I was hot as fish grease, and it would be hard to calm me down when I'm like this. I work, take care of my kids, and keep to myself. I don't know why people think shit sweet and like to fuck with me.

"Get the fuck off me. This is all your fault," I pointed out to Chase.

He wouldn't let me go, so I reached back and punched him in his right eye so he would have a matching black eye to go with the left one. He reached out his hand like he was about to hit me again but by this time, Martez was out there where we was.

"Man, I wish the fuck you would put your hands on my sister. I'll lay your ass out right here on this floor," Tez threatened.

"Don't be threating my son, the little bitch should've kept her hands to herself," Juliet stated, jumping in.

Juliet picked the wrong time to say something out of

pocket. I was pissed off and at this point, I didn't give two fucks about her being Chase's mother.

"I am about tired of your shit. Chase is your son, not your man. If you weren't such a bitch, you'd probably have a man of your own. What me and your son have going on is none of your business. You have all this misplaced hatred toward me when everything that is going on is the bastard that you birthed fault. You should've swallowed that motherfucker, then we wouldn't be having this problem right now. Let's not have to have this conversation again," I snapped.

"MCKENZIE, THAT'S ENOUGH!" my father bellowed, causing me to jump. My father rarely raises his voice at me, and when he did that meant he was serious. He and Martez were the only two people on this earth that I feared and if they raised their voice, I knew it meant for me to calm the fuck down and do as they say.

I already proved my point with everyone that I needed to, so there wasn't nothing else for me to do or say to them anyway. I hoped they took heed to what happened and leave me the fuck alone. I turned to walk away and ran right into Diane, who had a confused look on her face. I'm guessing she just got back because I hadn't seen her all day, so that meant she had no idea what had just taken place.

"Hey, just so you know, Shavon and Chase fucked in y'all house," I informed her as I walked away. What I said wasn't out of malice. She was a victim of circumstance like me and in a funny way, I felt bad for her. They were the two people she trusted and loved most in this world. She deserved to know what they were doing behind her back and not being left in the dark. Now what she did with this information was up to her. I did my part and I wasn't going to speak on it again.

I headed toward the kitchen and got a Ziplock bag. I filled it up with ice and held it on my bruised knuckles. My hand was hurting bad as hell. It felt like I had fractured my shit. I was praying I didn't because it was going to be hard as hell to do stuff with my kids since it's my right hand.

"Let me see your hand," my father stated, causing me jump.

I turned around and took the ice pack off and showed it to him. He took my hand into his and squeeze it lightly, instantly making me wince.

"Go put on some clothes and get a first-aid kit then meet me in my room," he said before walking off.

I went upstairs to my room and threw on the first pair of shorts and shirt I saw then grabbed the first-aid kit from my bag and went to his room. This time I made sure to knock before walking in.

I sat on the bed and handed him the first-aid kit. He wrapped my hand up then examined the scratches on my arms and neck. There was a bruise on my face from where Chase slapped me, but I would dare tell him Chase did that. It was my fault for punching him in the eye first and let's be real, at the end of the day, he's my kids' father and they need him.

"What was that about? Are you alright?" my father asked after nursing all of my wounds.

I told my dad everything that happened in the pool area, not leaving out one detail, before I broke down crying.

"I don't know what to do, Papa. I tried to make it work for the kids, but I'm tired. I can't do this anymore. I gave him another chance and he's still keeping secrets from me," I cried.

"Mija, you know I try to stay out of your personal affairs because if it was up to me, no guy would be able to date you, but I'm going to give my opinion and it's up to you to decide on what to do. Chase is not the guy for you. Unfortunately, he's the father of my grandkids so I can only wish the best for him, and from what you said, he's a good father. He reminds me a lot of myself when I was his age, and I would never want you to end up with a me. You're settling with him because you're upset with Blaze, and that's not right. You're physically with Chase but your heart is still with Blaze. It's okay for you to be single until you figure out what you want to do. You know your brother and I are here for you, and we'll help you out in any way you want us to."

"I just miss him so much, but I'm scared to open up to him again only for him to leave," I admitted for the first time as I cried into my father's chest. I had been conflicted with my feelings for Blaze and I never admitted to anyone how much I missed him.

"I've had conversations with Blaze since he's been away. I'm not going to tell you what we discussed because he told me in confidence, but I can say he misses you too. Your brother's wedding is next month and you know he'll be there. That's how much time you have to figure out what you want to do. Whether you want to get back with him or end things for good, you have to talk to him. It's time that you stop running from your problems," he told me.

I stayed in the room with my father, talking to him like I used to do when I was a teenager. I didn't go to my room because I knew Chase would come in there with his excuses and apologies, and I didn't want to hear it. This is the last place he would step foot in. Even if he tried to come in here, my dad would stop him.

CHAPTER ELEVEN
DIANE

Words can't explain how I felt hearing Kenzie tell me Chase and Shavon had sex in our house. I just knew she was lying and saying something to start some shit. There was no way Shavon and Chase would do some shit like that. I know Chase does his dirt, but he's never touched my family. Hell, him and Shavon don't even get along.

I turned around to look at Chase and Shavon. Neither of them even bothered denying what she said. Nor did they look me in the eyes. I just know this has to be some kind of sick joke. I felt like I was about to throw up where I stood. I was shaken up and tears started to form in my eyes. I literally have no one in this world but them, and they chose to betray me.

I watched as Chase walked my way, and a sense of relief washed over me. I thought he was coming to console. To reassure me that he would never do anything like that even if we're not together but instead, he kept walking right past me. I'm assuming to go talk to Kenzie, but it's not happening this time. I let him get away with a lot of shit while we were together, but not this time. I deserved to know what the fuck is going on.

I stormed in the house and up the stairs right behind him. I didn't care if he was going to his room or not. Kenzie could stand there and hear this entire conversation, if need be, but it was going to happen.

I turned the doorknob without knocking and pushed the door open. Chase was sitting on the bed with his face in his hands. He looked up at me, and all I saw was regret and sorrow in his eyes. Any other time I would have felt bad for him, but not this time. This time it was all about me and my feelings. Fuck him and the horse he rode in on.

"Chase, what the hell is Kenzie talking about? Tell me that she's lying," I begged.

Chase looked at me, and we must've stared at each other for at least five minutes in silence until he finally decided to speak.

"What Kenzie said is true, but she doesn't know the entire story. The shit didn't happen the way Shavon made it seem. We had sex the night she was at the house a few months ago after me and you had that argument about me never being at home anymore."

"You motherfucker, you had sex with her while I was in the house!" I yelled in disbelief as I charged at him. I swung on him, and he flung me out of the way like a rag doll.

"Don't put your hands on me, Diane, or I'm going to fuck you up. Either stand there and listen to what I have to say or get the fuck out and never get an explanation, because this is the only chance you'll get one from me."

I didn't want to hear any excuses but at the same time, I needed to know what happened. There was no way I could go on without knowing what happened from both of them.

"Okay, go ahead, and I want every detail," I told him.

"I'm not going into every detail, but a long story short, I had a lot on my mind so I was drinking and smoking before I went to bed. It was the middle of the night and dark as hell in the room. You know how hard I sleep when I'm drunk. I woke up with Shavon riding my dick. I thought you woke up and stopped being mad at me, so I laid back and enjoyed the shit. She didn't say anything and the only thing I did was grip her ass while she did her thing. It wasn't until I nutted that she finally opened her mouth. I had sobered the fuck up after that and pushed her ass off of me. I slapped her around a couple times. She told me that if I told you that you wouldn't believe me and she'd say I forced myself on her. I was going to tell you, but that's the only family you're close to so I was trying not to hurt you," he explained, and hearing his story only further pissed me off.

"You're a liar, of course you would blame it on her. My cousin wouldn't do no shit like that to me."

"Man, get the fuck out of my room. I don't have shit to gain or lose by lying to your ass about this. You know your cousin is a ho and has no problem fucking niggas that's unavailable. It just goes to show that you weren't an exception."

Chase was right, he didn't have a reason to lie to me now, but he was still wrong for keeping this shit from me. I love him and I would have found a way to believe and forgive him had he told me the truth when it happened.

Instead of saying anything else to Chase, I stormed out of the room and into the room I was sharing with Shavon. She was standing in front of the mirror cleaning her wounds. Kenzie had fucked her face up bad. At least this time she didn't have to go to the hospital. You'd think she would have learned by now to leave Kenzie alone. It's almost like she gets a thrill off getting her ass beat.

"What happened between you and Chase?" I asked.

"Do you see my fucking face right now? I'm not in the

mood to talk about that shit. This bitch fucked up my face again."

"I get this is bad timing, but I need to know your side of story. Please tell me that what Chase told me isn't true."

Shavon sighed then turned to look at me.

"You want to know what happened? Fine, you asked for it. Chase was drunk and I fucked him. I was so tired of hearing you bitch about what he was putting you through, but yet you was still fucking him and at his beck and call. I figured it had to be the dick, so I had to know for myself if it was worth it and babyyyy, he didn't even put in any work and he got me wanting more. I guess I see why you let him keep coming back. I'd be a dumb bitch for that nigga too. You and Kenzie are some lucky bitches. It was just sex, though, and I didn't think it was a big deal since y'all weren't together anymore." Shavon shrugged as she applied ice to her bloody lip. I couldn't believe she had the audacity to tell me this shit with a straight face.

"Bullshit, you knew I wouldn't be okay with you fucking him whether we were together or not. If that was the case, you would have told me what happened. We're family, and I thought I could trust you."

"Boo fucking hoo, that's what your problem is now, cousin. You're too fucking trusting. Chase showed you over and over again that he didn't want you and you couldn't trust him, but yet you come running back like a puppy with its tail between its legs even when he got that bitch pregnant. You're not built for a nigga like Chase. You're too fucking weak with no back bone," she ranted.

No lie, the shit coming out of Shavon's mouth broke my heart more than knowing that she fucked Chase. I couldn't give her the satisfaction of seeing me cry, but Lord knows I wanted to cry like a newborn baby fresh out of its mother's womb. Instead of entertaining Shavon's bullshit, I packed my suitcase and left the room.

I stood in front of the house and ordered my Uber. I was glad when I saw that it was only five minutes away. I couldn't get away from this hellhole fast enough.

The Uber came and took me to the airport. I got in line so I could change my flight for a standby one. It was my lucky day because there was a flight leaving in an hour. I hurriedly went through security with a couple minutes to spare. I was on autopilot as I boarded the plane. I popped a couple Tylenol to help with the headache that I felt coming and went to sleep. The flight wasn't long, so as quick as I was sleep, I was woke.

Once I landed, I Ubered to the house I once shared with Chase and finished packing my things. Chase was driving home whenever he decided to leave so either way, I had at least a nine-hour head start on him, but the sad thing about this is I doubt he'll even come back here anytime soon. He's going to be too busy trying to make right with Kenzie, and as much as I want to be mad about that, I can't because he will forever have ties with her through those kids. If they're not on speaking terms that means he's not updated with their lives, and I know they mean the world to him.

The good thing about all of this is that I found an apartment and got my keys the same day I flew out to Memphis. I planned on moving in on Monday, but I guess I'll get a head start on it now. I thought about if I should call Justin to come help me but as quick as the thought came, it left. I can't be that girl anymore. I needed to learn how to do stuff on my own and never become dependent on a man again. I can't allow anyone to ever be able to break me like this again. I've never felt so low in my life. I know this new journey I'm going to take will be hard, but it has to be worth it. I have to learn to love myself more, then maybe someday a man can love me the same way. I can't say I'll never get back with Chase again because him sleeping with Shavon wasn't his fault. I just hate he never told me about it. I have a love for him that may never die. I can say one thing, though, if I ever get back with him, I won't make it easy. He's going to have to work hard to prove to me that he can be the man I once thought I knew.

I packed for about two hours before I started loading my car. I didn't have a lot to take with me except my clothes and shoes. When I moved in with Chase his house was fully furnished, so I put all my things in storage. Once we got a bigger house, we were going to furnish the basement with my things. Sometime next week I'll rent a truck and have a couple movers get all of my things from storage and put them in my apartment.

My apartment is nowhere near as fancy as Chase's house and I'm fine with that. I make decent money at work so I won't struggle. I'm no longer in Schaumburg but I'm not in the hood either, so I'll be good. I'm actually ten minutes away from my job in Melrose Park. I'm hoping to stay here for a year and save as much as I can so by this time next year, I'll have my own house. It's time that I live my life to the fullest with no apologies.

CHAPTER TWELVE

CHASE

W e've been back from Memphis for almost two weeks now and I haven't heard from Kenzie since we left Memphis. We stayed there until Saturday as planned, but she didn't give me a chance to explain what happened between me and Shavon. I let her sleep in the room we shared and I slept in one of the other rooms to give her some space.

We rode back to Chicago together and that ride was awkward as hell. Kenzie was quiet the entire time and Tori looked like she wanted to stab me every time I looked in her direction. Since Kenzie isn't answering my calls, I'm on my way to her house now to talk to her. She allowed the twins to go back to Miami with her family because she said she needed a mental break. Her hand was also wrapped up, so it was going to be hard to maintain things with the kids on her own when Tori wasn't around. I told her that I could come there and be with them, but she just brushed me off. I've been able to see my kids through FaceTime whenever I call Tez or Lauren, but

I'm not about to do this forever. Even if Kenzie and I don't work things out, I need to be there for my kids.

I pulled up to Kenzie's house and rang the doorbell. I stood there for almost three minutes and was about to ring it again when she finally opened it in a pair of short biker shorts and a sports bra. Her hair was dripping water, so I guess she was in the middle of washing it when I showed up.

My eyes trailed her body and I tried my best not stare, but I couldn't help it. She looked good as hell in her natural state with no makeup and hair not done.

"Chase, why are you here? And stop staring at me, because it's not going to happen."

"I came so we can talk. It's been two weeks and we need to come to a common ground for the sake of our kids."

"Come in, I was actually going to call you anyway later on today because I'm flying out to Miami in the morning. I miss my kids and it's just a couple days earlier than when I was originally going anyway. "

"Okay, so when I slept with Shavon, me and you weren't together. I haven't touched another female since we got back together."

"I don't care if we were together or not, Chase. Even though I can't stand the damn girl, she's still my stepsister, and even if she wasn't my stepsister that's your ex's cousin. Plus, off the principle of me and her not getting along, that should have been enough for you to not even go there with her."

"You have to believe me when I say it wasn't like that. I would never do no shit like that to you or Diane. I don't even like Shavon's bird ass. I have black-out curtains in my room. I was drunk and passed out. When I woke up, she was riding me. I thought she was Diane so I just laid there the entire time until we were finished. I didn't touch her or nothing so I couldn't tell the difference until she opened her mouth and said something. At that point, I smacked her around. I know I'm wrong for not telling you, but I thought you wouldn't believe me," I admitted.

"Whether you thought I would believe you or not, you should have told me. I said no more secrets or surprises."

"I thought you meant from now on that we're back together," I said honestly.

"You know what, it don't even matter if I believe you or not. We can never get back together again. Just me knowing that you fucked her makes me sick to my stomach because I know how she gets down. I hope you got your ass checked, because that's the first thing I did when I got back here."

"Kenzie, that was I don't know how many months ago and besides, I strapped up every time me and you had sex since then."

"I'm not taking any chances. You weren't strapped up when you was eating my pussy or me sucking your dick."

Kenzie was right about that. I'm so used to using condoms that I forget to get my regularly checkups, not thinking about the shit I can catch just from getting my dick sucked. I'm not lying to Kenzie when I say she's the only one I've been with since we got back together. She gives me head on the regular, so I don't need to go off and get my dick sucked from somebody else in the process.

"Okay, you're right. I know that you're not fucking with me like that, but what are we going to do about Christmas? I don't want to kiss my kids' first Christmas. I can skip your brother's wedding if you want me to, but I want to come down there and spend time with my kids for Christmas. I will stay in a hotel if I have to."

"It's up to you if you want to still come to the wedding or not. Just know we'll be going together as friends and you'll be making this trip for our kids. There will be no elaborate scheme of us getting back together, because it's not happening. You don't have to book a room. You can stay at the house just in your own room or in the twins' room. There's a futon in there."

"Okay, I'll be there for the wedding then so I can spend more time with the kids. I know I'm not your favorite person right now and you don't have to do this, but I appreciate you doing this for me."

"Let's get something straight. I'm not doing this for you. I'm doing it for my kids. No matter what we go through, at the end of the day, you're their father and they deserve to have you in their life. When we come back from Miami you can come get them every other weekend to spend the night and you can come by three days out of the week to visit. When I say you can get them on the weekend, I do mean you. Not your mother, brother, or Diane. If I call you, I expect to see you with my kids."

I didn't want to resort to seeing my kids a couple hours out of the week after seeing them every day, but I'll do what I have to do for now.

"Okay, and you don't have to worry about me leaving them with Diane. When I made it back from Memphis, she had moved most of her things out already. She has her own apartment and I live at the house on my own."

"Alright, we've talked about everything that we need to talk about, so you should go now. I have to finish packing because I have an early morning flight."

I wasn't ready to leave. I wanted to find something else to talk about just so I could talk to her a little longer. She didn't tell me to get my things out of her house, so I looked at this as just a way of her saying she needs space and that there might be a shot for us after all.

I didn't want to push my luck, though, and bring it up, so I left her house like she requested and headed to my warehouse. That's where I've been for the last two weeks. I've been working my ass off making sure everything runs smoothly. I'm going to spend a couple hours there then I have some other business to take care of.

It took me damn near an hour to get to the warehouse due to traffic. When I got there my men were already unloading trucks and some were cutting up dope. I had a room set for each task. Me and Tino also have our own offices with showers and futons in them. It comes in handy for those late nights here at the warehouse when we're waiting on drop-offs and pickups. I don't even go to the trap anymore unless I'm dropping off work or doing a drop by to make sure those niggas taking care of business. We left Quan and K.G. in charge of our main trap, but those niggas be needing to be checked on too. Lately, both of their asses have been slacking. They're both more interested in chasing behind hoes than they are about taking care of business. I don't know why the fuck Quan so wrapped up in Shavon's ass. He knows that she's a ho and that she fucked me, but that ain't stopping him from fucking with her. For his sake, I hope he's strapping up and Aniyah doesn't find out, or she's going to kill his ass.

I went to my office and starting going over the details for my next shipment. Getting this warehouse was the best thing I could do for my business. We're selling way more kilos now than we ever have. I've been stacking my money and making sure to put a nice amount in a savings account for my kids so that if anything ever happens to me, they'll be well taken care of.

I was almost done with my work when my phone started ringing. I looked down at it and saw that it was Bri.

"Hello," I answered.

"Hey baby, you're still playing house with your baby mama or you ready to come see me?"

"I can't, I'm working right now. What you need though?"

"I'm trying to get my hair and nails done."

"Oh, you must be trying to do more than suck some dick?"

"You know I'm always down to fuck. You're the one that always just wants your dick sucked."

"Aight, I got you. I'll tell you where to meet me when I'm done."

"Okay, don't try to play me either because I'll be waiting for you."

"I said I got you, just wait for my call," I told her before hanging up.

I haven't had sex in over two weeks and technically I'm single now, so I don't know when I'm going to get some more pussy, so I might as well fuck Bri and have her help remove this stress.

I put my phone back in my pocket and got up to get ready. I put on my bulletproof vest and grabbed my black jacket and guns then left the room. When I made it to the front, Tino, Quan, and Mike were waiting for me.

"Let's go get this shit over with," I said.

We all left the warehouse and climbed in a black van. The spot we were hitting up was about twenty minutes from the warehouse.

"You good, bro?" Tino asked.

"Yeah, I went by Kenzie's and talked to her for a minute. I'm going to still go out to Miami for the wedding."

"Okay, so y'all back cool now?" Quan inquired.

"If by cool you mean we're going to have a healthy coparent-ship, then yeah. She wouldn't even discuss us working on getting back together. I'm just going to give her space and let her figure out what she wants to do."

We pulled up to the front of the house and jumped out of the van. My driver stayed in with it running so he can pull right off when we come out.

"Quan, come with me through the back," I told him.

"We're going through the front now," Tino added.

"Get y'all bitch asses on the floor now," Mike yelled as he waved his gun around.

We ran around to the back, making sure our masks were secure before kicking in the door.

"Where's Nardo?" I yelled.

"He's not here right now. We haven't seen him in almost a week," one of the guys said.

"Tell his bitch ass Raymond wants to talk to him!" I yelled while the guys bagged up all the dope and money they could see.

One of the niggas tried to be slick and dial something on their phone, so I shot his ass in the hand then pistol whipped him. This was only supposed to be a robbery, but we couldn't afford for anyone to come before we left.

We ran out of the building and to the van. The driver sped away and we got to counting the money during the drive.

By the time we made it to the warehouse, we'd counted eighty thousand dollars in cash. That meant we get twenty thousand apiece, on top of the twenty thousand each that Raymond paid us for doing the job. All the dope was going back to him since it was his to begin with. Some niggas hit up one of his traps and he paid us to get the drugs back for him. We don't do this kind of job on the regular, but it's a way to make some quick money, and I owed Raymond a favor for something he did for me a while back.

I went to my office and put my money in a safe then texted Bri and told her to meet me at my old house. I don't feel like going to the trap and I'm not getting a room just for a quick fuck. I'm about to get my nut off then send her about her way. Even though I live by myself now, my house in Schaumburg is still my safe house where no one will know where I live. Especially since that's the place I'll be at with my kids.

By the time I made it to the house, Bri's thirsty ass was already parked out front. I don't know where she came from, but I wasn't expecting her here so soon. I got out of my car and used my keys to let myself in the house. She followed behind me as I walked to my room. As soon as the door closed, Bri wasted no time dropping to her knees. She pulled down my jogging pants and got to work. I held the back of her head and fucked her throat until she was swallowing my seeds. She stayed down there and sucked it back to life while playing in her pussy.

Once I was hard, I pushed her away and grabbed a condom from the nightstand then rolled it on.

Bri already knew how I got down, so she only lifted her dress over her ass and bent over the bed. I wasn't going to kiss or make love to her, so this was the only position she was going to get. Twenty minutes later, she was on her third nut and I had my second one. She left the room to go to the bathroom to freshen up, and I reached in my pocket and grabbed three hundred dollars.

I walked to the bathroom with my pants around my ankles and cleaned my dick. I pulled my pants up and gave her the money, then we left the house together, going our separate ways. That's what I like about Bri. She don't want to have conversations or even go out. All she want to do is suck my dick and get paid. It might look like I'm tricking, but I don't give a fuck. I look at it as having a peace of mind and a nut with no hassle. That's hard to come around these days because bitches be wanting girlfriend privileges with ho duties.

I drove straight home so I can shower and go to sleep. I'll have an early morning tomorrow since I'm going to be gone for over a week. I need to make sure everything is straight before I leave so that I'm not interrupted while away.

CHAPTER THIRTEEN
BLAZE

My therapy ended last week and I'm feeling better than ever, just in time for my trip to Miami. I just finished packing the last of my things and I can't wait to see McKenzie's reaction when she sees me for the first time in person since I left eight months ago. Just thinking about how long this took pisses me off. I never thought I'd be away this long. Getting shot fucked up my plans big time. I pray she still feels the same way she did when I left, or at least close to it. I'll hate to have to go out there and kidnap her little ass.

I pulled off my pants and shirt then climbed in bed. As soon as my head touched the pillow, my phone started to ring. I looked down at it and saw that it was Akina. I haven't talked to her since the last day of my therapy and she's been blowing up my phone since. I have no idea why, but I'm going to answer now because by the time I board that flight to Miami tomorrow, she'll be blocked.

"Hey," I answered dryly, hoping she gets the hint.

"Hey, I've been calling you all week. Let me find out you're acting funny with me now that we've had sex," she stated.

"I'm not acting funny with you. You wanted some dick so I gave it to you. What else do you want from me? Because I don't have anything to give," I replied.

Akina came over two days later for my therapy session after she gave me head and instead of us working out like we usually do, we fucked for the hour. Afterward, I let her leave and when she came back the week after for another session, she thought we were going to fuck, but I shot her down. I needed to work out to make sure everything was straight with me, so she needed to do her job. She tried to convince me to come to her house afterward, but I didn't know her like that.

Akina had some good pussy, but it wasn't good enough for me to continue fucking her. I didn't touch her that way again because I didn't need her getting attached but apparently, one time is all it takes for her to get in her feelings.

"Damn, you don't have to say it like that. I just thought that maybe we could go somewhere and get to know each other better since our sessions are over. You won't be mixing business with pleasure, so there's nothing in our way unless you lied about not being in a relationship with Kim and Tasia."

"Baby girl, I'm many things, but a liar ain't one. I don't even mess with either of them anymore. I'm leaving Cali tomorrow and going to Miami, and then from there I'm going back home for good, hopefully with the woman I plan to spend the rest of my life with."

"Wow, so you're engaged?"

"Not yet, but I plan on being soon."

"So I guess this is it? You used me and now I won't hear from you again?"

I sighed because this girl was really starting to get on my

damn nerves. I'm trying hard not to curse her out, but she's pushing it.

"How the fuck did I use you? I had no intentions on even sticking my dick in you until you started throwing the pussy at me. I'm a nigga, so I caught the shit. I gave you what you wanted. I didn't sell you any hopes or dreams of us ever being together, so gone somewhere with this bullshit."

"Whatever, you didn't stop me from sucking your dick that day and you were the one that made the first move we fucked."

"The fuck I look like stopping you while my dick in your mouth? I'm about to hang up now though, cuz this conversation is pointless and I have to get up in the morning," I told her before hanging up the phone and blocking her. I'm not even going to bother about waiting until I get on the plane.

I put my phone on the nightstand and closed my eyes before going to sleep. I was sleeping good as hell until I was awakened by somebody massaging my dick. I turned on the light and jumped out of the bed.

"What the fuck are you doing in here, Tasia? You know I'm not fucking with you like that anymore."

"Yeah, you said that, but I don't see why. What's going on in Miami that I have to wait until Christmas to come down there? Lauren's wedding isn't until next week, so why are you going out there now?"

"I told you I have some shit to take care of."

I broke things off with both Tasia and Kim last week without explanation. Just that it was fun while it lasted, but I'm going back to Chicago and everyone has their own house there. Let's just say neither of them took it well. I've had to sleep with my door locked every night to keep them from coming in my bed and raping me.

"Okay, so can I at least go to the wedding? You're taking my daughter with you."

"There's a headcount for the wedding and I didn't RSVP for a plus one."

"Yeah alright, I bet this has to do with that bitch, Kenzie. I know she's going to be at the wedding and she's probably already in Miami."

"Tasia, we were never together. I don't have to explain myself to you, now get out of my room so I can get ready and go. I'll see you when y'all get to Miami."

We're all spending Christmas in Miami since Lauren's wedding is there. Tamika and her husband Carl are even coming out here. This will be the first time we all spent Christmas in one household. We're not doing how Kenzie's family did though. Tamika, Carl, and the kids are staying at a hotel while Mason, Myra, Tasia, Kim, and the kids are staying at the safe house. Meanwhile, I'll be spending the night at Kenzie's parents' house. She just doesn't know it yet.

"Fuck you and that bitch, Blaze. You better hope I don't come to Miami and catch you with that young ho," Tasia spat.

I instantly reached out and grabbed the front of Tasia's shirt. She knows I don't take threats or disrespect lightly.

"Watch your motherfucking mouth before I fuck you up. If you see me with Kenzie, you'll either keep it moving or you'll speak to us. I wish she would tell me you tried some shit with her, it'll be a problem," I threatened her.

"Wow, I see how it is," Tasia said before walking out of the room.

I looked over at the clock and decided to get dressed. There was no point of me lying back down since my alarm was set to go off in thirty minutes anyway. I went in the bathroom and took a hot shower then put on a pair of jogging pants and a t-shirt with a pair of sneakers.

Once I was done, I chopped it up with Mason for a little while then headed to the airport. I checked in two suitcases and still had a carryon with a personal item. I was taking everything I had bought during the time I was away because I didn't know when I was going back to Cali.

Six hours later, I was landing in Miami. I got my luggage and headed to Tez's parked car. He picked me up because Lauren took Kenzie with her to run around so I can surprise her when they get home.

"What's up, man?" I spoke.

"What's going on? You ready to see my sister?"

"Yeah, but no lie, I'm nervous as hell. She might try to beat my ass."

"Maybe, she's been on a roll lately, but you better be ready to make things right with her and be completely honest about what's been going on with you. Don't make me regret helping you get her back."

"You don't have to worry about that, and I ended everything I had going on while I was away. I'm ready to be with her and start a future," I admitted.

"Okay, well Isabella set up everything for you already, so you just have to pick up the food. Lauren already ordered what you wanted so give them her name."

"Thank you, I appreciate this."

"Don't thank me yet, you have to wait and see if it works."

"It'll work, it has to work," I said to myself more than him.

Tez dropped me off at the safe house and I transferred my bags from his car to mine, then I went to the florist shop to pick out some flowers. After that, I went to the restaurant to get the food. I was going to have a picnic with Kenzie in their garden while we discuss everything that's been going on.

When I made it to Kenzie's house, I gave the food to Isabella so she could finish setting up while I changed into a pair of black jean shorts with a red polo shirt and a pair of red and black Air Max. By the time I was done, Tez told me Kenzie and Lauren were pulling up.

I went out back and waited for Kenzie at the table that was set up for us. Isabella had a fruit tray and a bottle of red wine on the table.

I sat there nervous as hell for what felt like an eternity when it was probably only five minutes. When Kenzie came out, my breath was caught in my throat. She had on a short halter top that showed off her long thick legs with a pair of gladiator sandals. Her hair was in its natural curls and she had on a light coat of nude lipstick. I wanted to go run and pick her up, but I maintained my composure and stood up from the table to hold her chair out for her.

Kenzie finally walked over and surprised me by wrapping her arms around me. I let out the breath I was holding as I held her tightly. We stayed that way for I don't know how long, until she finally let me go. She stepped back and looked at me before reaching out and slapping the hell out of me. Now that was the reaction I was expecting from her.

"You motherfucker, you break up with me to keep me safe only to get shot and tell me not to come see you because of some other bitches, and now you show up here like everything is all good with a fucking picnic," she snapped.

"I know it's not all good, and I regretted telling you not come see me the minute you hung up the phone on me. You have to know that I'm sorry and I'll never leave you like this again. I love you, Kenzie, and I'm willing to do whatever you want for me to make things right between us."

"Okay, you want to make things right and work on us. Let's put everything on the table now. Tell me what the fuck you been doing besides being in the streets," Kenzie said before sitting down.

I sat across from Kenzie and poured her a glass of wine because she was going to need it.

"When I left it had nothing to do with Tasia. I ended up sleeping with her a couple times when I went to Miami to see my daughter, but then I stopped. I went back to Cali and while there, Kim came and worked for me. I started sleeping with her instead. The night I called you, I planned on ending things with Kim but then I was shot. I didn't plan on sleeping with them again, but then I saw all those pictures of you with Chase and I thought, fuck it. Kim, Tasia and I ended up in a three-way situation. I also slept with my physical therapist once, but I ended everything with all of them last week. I want it to just be me and you from now on. I don't want to play games anymore. I don't care if you was sleeping with Chase or anybody else as long as you cut the shit off and be with me. I know all of this is my fault and I brought it upon myself."

"I want to be mad at you right now, but I can't. I missed the shit out of you and used Chase as a void. I ended things with him the day after Christmas because he's a fucking liar that likes to hide shit from me. He's still coming out here for the wedding and Christmas, though, to spend time with the twins. I want to believe that we can work on things, but I'm scared, Malakai. You made me fall in love for you only to up and leave me. How do I know some more shit won't go down in the streets and you'll have to leave me again?"

"I promise I'll never leave you again unless it's my only option. All the beef I had in the street is over now. I'm just trying to build businesses and make money. I plan on giving all this shit up in a couple years, then me, you, and our kids and future kids will be set for life."

"Future kids, huh?" Kenzie asked with a raised eyebrow.

"Yes, I plan on giving you my last name then planting my seed in you on our honeymoon," I told her seriously.

"Who said I want your last name or baby?" she countered.

"Oh, you do," I said with confidence.

Kenzie and I ended up talking about our old memories and the good times we had together. I told her about some of the stuff I had to do while I was away, and she told me about the accomplishments she made while I was away. I can't wait to see the twins. They're with her aunt Victoria for the weekend since the bachelor and bachelorette parties are taking place tomorrow.

We stayed outside until we were finished eating then headed inside the house together.

"We can watch a movie if you want to, unless you have plans," Kenzie offered.

"The only plans I have are being here with you tonight. Just so you know, I planned on staying here in your bed whether you wanted to get back with me or not. All of my clothes are in my trunk and I'm staying here until you go back to Chicago, then I'm going with you."

"Okay, so what if I was still with Chase when I came out here, then what was your plans?"

"Girl, I don't give a fuck about that nigga. I was still going to stay in this house. I would've slept in another room but before this trip was over, you were going to be mine again."

"Your confidence is sexy, but I'm not letting you off the hook that easily. You can sleep in the bed with me tonight, but we're not having sex. When was the last time you were checked out?"

"Last week, and I haven't been with any of them since," I said. I reached in my pocket and pulled out the test results, handing them to her.

Kenzie took the paper and ran it over then handed it back to me.

"We're still not fucking, but we can go up and watch a movie."

"That's fine, we don't have to do anything until you're ready. I'm not going anywhere, so there's no need to rush."

Kenzie and I undressed down to our underwear then climbed in her bed. She turned on *365 Days* then snuggled up under me. She knew what she was doing by turning this damn movie on and saying I can't touch her. She was trying to test me, but I was going to restrain myself and not touch her. Halfway through the movie she was already sleep, so I turned it off. There was no way I was going to watch this without her. I was tired since I didn't get much sleep, so I kissed her on the forehead and went to sleep myself.

CHAPTER FOURTEEN

MCKENZIE

The following morning, I woke up engulfed in Malakai's strong arms. His grip was tight as hell, like he was scared I was going to leave him in the middle of the night. He always held me like this when we slept in the bed together, even before we started dating. I can't lie; lying here in his arms felt like home. I didn't realize how much I missed being held securely until last night. Chase and I cuddled sometimes but he never held me tightly. I could easily ease out of his arms and he wouldn't notice. Most of the time, I only laid on him for a little and by the time we woke up, we were on separate sides of the bed.

Malakai's erect manhood was poking me in the back. I wanted to grind on him so bad and just let him stick it in, but I couldn't let him off the hook that easy. I didn't want him to think that sex would make everything right. I'm not even mad at him anymore because I had a chance to sit back and put myself in his shoes. If someone was after me and my kids were in danger from it, I wouldn't hesitate to leave them with someone else that would be able to keep them safe. I also thought about the conversation I had with my father. It was time for me to stop running away from my problems. I'm getting too old for this shit. If I ever want a stable adult relationship, I have to learn how to listen and communicate.

I was lowkey feeling some type of way about him fucking with Tasia and Kim. I didn't care about the physical therapist because she was someone he was never going to see again. I already know we're going to have problems from Kim and Tasia because neither of them is over him. I'm going to keep it cool, though, as long as they stay in their lane. All I know is that he better be done with them for good, though, because if I find out he's still fucking around with them, I'm going to go across his head with something.

I laid here for almost twenty minutes trying to see if Malakai's going to wake up on his own. My bladder feels like it's about to burst and he isn't budging. I can't hold it any longer, so I wiggled some to get out of his arms and the whole time, I was rubbing against his dick.

"It's taking all of my self-control not whip my dick out and stick it in you, Kenzie, so be still," Malakai warned me in a husky tone. His morning voice had my pussy dripping wet, and I needed to hurry up and get my ass out this bed before I take him up on his offer.

"I'm sorry, I was trying to get out of your arms so I can go to the bathroom, but your ass heavy as hell," I replied.

Malakai lifted one of his arms and I slid out from under him. I rushed inside of the bathroom and released my bladder. I brushed my teeth while I was in there then put on a robe. I walked out of the bathroom and Malakai had already fallen back to sleep. I needed somebody to talk to about my situation, so I left the room and walked down the hall to Lauren and Martez's room. I knocked on the door and Lauren yelled come in.

I pushed the door open, and she was sitting up in bed looking through a magazine while Martez was still asleep.

"What's up, mamas?"

"Hey babez, I need some girl talk," I told her.

Lauren slid over to the middle of their king size bed, and she tapped the spot next to her.

I walked over and climbed in the bed next to her.

"What's wrong? Does this have anything to do with my cousin spending the night with you last night?" she asked.

"Yes, we had a long talk yesterday over dinner and he says he wants to get back together. I want to get back with him and he's willing to take things at my pace, but what if I'm making the wrong decision? He was fucking Kim and Tasia during our break, so I already know it's going to be some bullshit when they find out we're together. What if he gets mad at me or something and decides to fuck one of them again? Then you know what I went through with Chase, not to mention we just broke up last month. What if people think I'm a ho or something from jumping between them?"

"First of all, my cousin is not Chase. If he still wanted to fuck with Kim and Tasia, he wouldn't have left them in Cali and came to you. Secondly, fuck what anybody thinks. You deserve to be happy and if Blaze can give you that, then be with him. You already know I'm team Blaze and I wish the hell Kim or any other bitch would try to give you any problems over him. I'll beat they ass and he'll put them in their place. He's not about to have you out here looking crazy fighting bitches because of him."

"I hear you, Lauren, but to be honest, I'm scared to open up to him and have sex only for him to leave me," I admitted. That was the part that fucked me up in the head and pissed me off the most with Malakai. We had went all that time without having sex only for him to leave the next day. That fucked up a bitch's pride and mind for real.

"Oh, Kenzie, that's not going to happen. If you feel that way, though, you need to talk to him and let him know. Make him reassure you that everything is going to be alright. I can't tell you when to sleep with him, and if you're not ready right now because of those feelings, then wait. He's my cousin, but you're my sister. If he can't wait or understand where you're coming from, then he's not the man I thought he was nor the man for you," Lauren advised me.

"Yeah, and I'll shoot his ass the next time he breaks your heart," Martez added. He turned and looked at me.

"Dude, I thought you were sleep. You eavesdropping on our girl talk?" I asked.

"Nah, I just woke up on the end of your conversation. I have to piss but I don't have on any clothes, so I was trying to give y'all a chance to finish talking before I kick your ass out of my room," he said.

"Ewww, I'll see you later, Lauren," I said, hopping out of their bed and running out of the room. I smiled as I walked back to my room. Talking to Lauren made me feel a lot better. She said a lot of things that I needed to hear.

I walked back in my bedroom, and it was empty. I knocked on my bathroom door and there was no answer, so I pushed it open. I didn't see Malakai, so I walked all the way in the bathroom and around to my shower area, and there he was, low and behold, in all his glory. I have a glass Fontana smart and intelligent LED shower head with a feature touch panel to control showerhead features. He had the shower head turned to the waterfall option that allowed the water to cover your entire body when you stand under it.

Malakai was stroking his thick dick with a soapy towel, and

his head was held back like that shit was feeling good as hell. Water cascaded down his body as he concentrated on what he was doing. My throat went dry and my kitty was thumping as I watched in awe. My hand traveled under my robe and found its way inside of my boy shorts. I rubbed my clit in a circular motion and a moan instantly left my mouth. I guess he heard me, because he stopped what he was doing and looked in my direction.

"Come here," he demanded as he slid the shower door open.

At this moment, the devil and angel were dancing on my shoulder, talking in my ears.

"Girl, it's too soon, you letting him off too easily if you give in now," the angel said.

"Bitch, don't listen to her. You only live once. Go jump on him and do a handstand before I do," the devil added.

I guess I was standing there too long without saying anything because before I knew it, Malakai had reached out and pulled me in the shower with him.

"Why did you do that? Now my robe and underwear is wet," I whined.

"You should've came over here like I told you to. I don't like repeating myself, McKenzie," he told me as he untied my robe and allowed it to fall on the floor.

Malakai wrapped his hand securely around my neck, and our lips connected as he pushed me against the shower wall. He slid his tongue in my mouth and a surge shot through my body down to my lower regions as we tongue wrestled. He broke the kiss and made his way to my neck where he started sucking gently. He unhooked my bra and it fell to the floor, and my boy shorts were right behind that.

He lifted one of my legs over his shoulder and started licking my inner thigh. This man had me ready to cum and he hasn't even touched my pussy yet. I needed to end this because I was serious about not fucking him yet.

"Malakai, I'm not about to fuck you. We still have some things to discuss first," I told him as my breath hitched in my throat. He had slid one of his fingers in my dripping pussy.

"I know, baby, just relax and let me make you cum. Can you do that for me?" he asked.

All I could do was nod my head because at that point, he had slid another finger in and was rubbing my clit with another one. I was a moaning mess as I came all over his hand.

Malakai removed his fingers and ran them across my lips, causing me to taste myself. He gripped my waist then flipped me upside down with both of my legs over his shoulders and started flicking his tongue against my pussy.

"Oh my god, Kai, please don't drop me," I managed to get out in between moans. He ignored me and continued his meal. I was eye level to his dick, so I thought, what the hell.

I held onto his legs as I licked up and down his dick before putting it in my mouth. As I sucked his dick, I could feel him humming in my pussy. The vibration of his tongue and his goatee pricking my love nest made me instantly bust all over his face.

"You be trying to get dropped sucking my dick that. Let me put you down so you can do you," he told me.

Malakai gently flipped me back over, and I pushed him up against the other wall as I dropped to my knees. He was standing there with his hands behind head, watching me make his dick disappear down my throat.

"God damn, Kenzie, you about to make me nut," he groaned.

I pulled him halfway out of my mouth and stroked his dick while sucking on his mushroom until his warm seeds were flowing down my throat.

I sucked a little more until he pushed me away because his shit was sensitive as hell. I got up from the floor and we finally showered, brushed our teeth, and got dressed. I wanted to stay locked up in my room talking to Malakai, but Lauren and Martez were waiting for us. We had to do the final fitting for the wedding and prepare for their joint bachelor and bachelorette party for tonight.

We all ran and took care of everything. By the time we made it back to the house it was five o'clock and I was tired as hell. All I wanted to do was take a quick nap, but I needed to make sure the back yard was set up for tonight. We hired a bartender, caterer, strippers, and a DJ. There's going to be games as well. I can't wait to see how it all turns out.

I'm Lauren's maid of honor and Martez's right-hand man, Don, is the best man, so we're in charge of tonight's events. We were supposed to pay for everything together, but he wouldn't take any money from me. He also didn't put any thought or effort into the event, so I guess it's a fair trade. All he said was, "I trust your judgment, lil' sis. Set up everything and tell me how much it costs."

The back yard is decorated with a black, red, and silver color scheme because that's the wedding colors. There were tables set up throughout the yard and a dance floor. Even though the party was for both of them, there was a divided section for the men and women when it came to play games.

Everything looked good, so I went upstairs to my bedroom so I could start getting ready. When I walked in, Malakai was laid across my bed knocked out sleep. He's never slept this much in the past, so I needed to know what was up.

I climbed in the bed and straddled him, causing him to flicker his eyes open.

"Damn, you want to pick up where we left off at this morning?" Malakai asked with a grin.

"No, do you have a baby on the way or some shit? I don't want no surprises down the line," I told him seriously.

"What? Why would you ask me some shit like that? I ain't just been out here wilding. I ain't been raw dogging nobody and I ain't no pussy. You was the last person I gave head to and the first in eight months."

"Then why are you sleeping so much?"

Malakai lifted me off of him and reached in his suitcase and tossed me a prescription bottle pill. I looked at it and saw that it was a bottle of Vicodin.

"I'm doing better but I'm not one hundred percent. I try not to take the pills every day but my leg was hurting. You don't have to worry about nobody else carrying my child except you."

"Okay, there better not be, because there's no way in hell I was going to be with you if you had a baby with Kim or another one with Tasia."

Malakai and I continued to catch up while I combed my hair, then we showered again. Once we were done, we got dressed and headed outside so we could greet the people as they came. There were a lot of half-naked women out here, and I'm not talking about the strippers. The guys couldn't keep their hands and eyes to themselves.

"So, Lauren, I see your fine ass cousin Blaze here. You think he ready to give me a shot now?" Lauren's friend Tyesha said as she eyed my man.

"Girl, that nigga ain't going. He not even entertaining the strippers," another female added.

I was about to respond when I felt somebody tap me on my shoulder. I turned around and saw some dude that I didn't recognize, but I'm assuming he's one of my brother's people, so I was not about to entertain him. Plus, Blaze was on the other side of the room burning a hole in me with his eyes.

"What's up, beautiful, do you want to dance?" he asked.

"No thank you, I'm good."

"Suit yourself, I'll be over there if you change your mind," he said, pointing in the direction of where a group of guys were standing.

"Damn girl, why you turn his fine ass down? Don't you know he has money?" the female who I didn't know said.

"Because I have a man, so I have no interest in entertaining my brother's friends."

"Girl, your brother's friends got bank," Tyesha jumped in.

"So do me and my man," I replied.

I stood with the girls talking for a few minutes until Blaze walked over to me and handed me a drink.

"Here, are you going to come chill with me so these females will leave me alone?" he whispered in my ear.

"Yeah, I guess I can mark my territory for little bit." I smirked.

Blaze pulled me close to him and tongued me down right there in front of everyone so they could know we both were off limits.

"Aye, get your hands off my sister," Martez yelled, causing both of us to laugh.

The rest of the night went great. I was glad we didn't have to clean anything. I took a shower because I was sticky from all that dancing, then joined Malakai in bed where we both passed out instantly.

CHAPTER FIFTEEN

CHASE

T he past two weeks I have been burying myself with work. Business is great and my money is getting longer. Even though I'm going to Miami for a wedding and the holidays, this is a much-needed vacation for me. All I do is make money and stack it, but I never go out and enjoy the fruits of my labor. I buy shit for my kids and Kenzie, but I don't buy lavish things for myself and I haven't been out of town for a trip unless it had to do with business.

I sent Tino and my mother a text letting them know I made it while I waited for my rental. I rented a black Lamborghini truck. I wanted a Ferrari but my kids' car seats can't fit in there. Once I was done with all the paperwork, I put the address McKenzie gave me in the GPS. I listened to Rick Ross as I hit the E-way. I was on there for about twenty minutes and then I got off. I drove down back roads for damn near ten minutes with no houses in sight. I thought my GPS was fucking up until I made it to a gate with security outside of it. I wasn't sure if I was at the right spot or not.

I rolled down my window and the guard approached my window.

"How can I help you?" he asked.

"Is this the Alvarez residence?"

"Yes, who are you here for?"

"I'm looking for McKenzie."

"Okay, what's your name?"

"Chase James."

He went inside his booth and pulled out a clipboard. He scanned it then returned.

"I need to see some identification first."

"Are you serious?" I asked.

"Yes, either you give me your ID or I can't permit you entrance."

I sighed and pulled my ID out of my wallet and handed it to him. This man pulled out a scanner and scanned it then wrote down something from my card before handing it to me. I had never seen no kind of shit like this at a home before. He went back to a booth and the tall gates opened. I drove around a winding lot for what felt like forever until I pulled up to this huge ass mansion with nothing but black trucks and foreign cars in the driveway.

I knew Kenzie's father's side of the family had money, but I didn't know the shit was this long. This motherfucking house made me feel like I wasn't working enough. McKenzie never told me what her father and brother did for a living. All she told me was they were business owners, and I let it go because it had nothing to do with me, but I know she left something out. There were two men packing heat standing at the front door of the house. Not to mention the cameras that are out here.

I parked next to one of the trucks and got out. I grabbed my bags from the trunk then walked up to the front door. The men nodded their heads at me but didn't say a word. I rang the doorbell and about two minutes later, the door swung open by who I'm assuming is the housekeeper since she had on the standard black and white maid uniform.

There was all kinds of hustle and bustle going on throughout the house. I guess with the wedding being tomorrow and Christmas the day after, they had a lot of planning and work to do.

"Hello sir, you can leave your bags right here and someone will take them up to your room. Follow me out to the back where Ms. Alvarez is."

I followed the housekeeper through the back of the house. There were chefs in the kitchen cooking and another maid cleaning up.

I don't know why McKenzie would ever come back to Chicago if she was living like this out here. No wonder her little spoiled ass wasn't easily impressed. She was living better than I could ever imagine in this lifetime.

We made it outside and people were scattered around setting up for the wedding. They had built an arch and had circle tables with chairs under them and a long table up front. If my garden looked like this, I would get married in it too.

I walked around the yard until I spotted McKenzie sitting on a blanket holding my son with Tamika, a man I didn't recognize, and Blaze. I had to do a double take when I saw him sitting there holding my daughter. I didn't even know him and Kenzie were still in contact. I forgot Lauren is his cousin, so it makes sense for him to be here since they were getting ready for the rehearsal dinner.

"What's up, y'all," I spoke, getting their attention.

They all spoke as I sat down next to Kenzie.

"Did anyone show you to your room?" Kenzie asked.

"No, but your housekeeper said someone would take my bags up to my room."

"Okay, when you're ready I'll show you to the twins' room. I told them to put your stuff in there because the only available guest rooms are out in the cottage house, but someone else will be sleeping in one of them and I figured you didn't want that. My father also expanded the house and put two bedrooms in the basement, but the help is staying in those."

"It's cool, I told you I don't mind sharing a bedroom with the kids."

Blaze leaned over and whispered something to Kenzie, and she nodded her head up and down with a smile.

I sat down and played with my son while everyone discussed their holiday plans. Blaze kept whispering in Kenzie's ear, and whatever he was saying had her showing all thirty-two teeth. They were looking real cozy together and had me wondering if they were back fucking around with each other. *Is he the reason she gave up on me so easily? Had she been talking to him behind my back while we were together? Was this part of her plan all along?* All kind of questions were going through my mind and I needed them answered.

"Aye, can you show me to my room?" I asked McKenzie.

"Yeah," she said, standing up from the ground.

Kenzie took Chance out of Blaze's arm and she led the way.

"This house is nice as hell. Why did you choose to live in Chicago? I can tell you're closer to your family here than out there."

"I didn't stay out here because of my mother. I didn't want her to think what she did for me wasn't enough. When I broke up with you and came out here, I was going to stay here for good until I found out I was pregnant. I thought you deserved a chance to be in your kids' life. Had you been a dead-beat dad, I would have been back here on the first thing smoking when my kids were able to fly."

"Okay, that's understandable."

"I'll give you a mini tour of the house as I show you the way to the room. Down the hall by the foyer where you came in at is the family room. The one on the left is the hall. That's where all the meals are served for breakfast, lunch, and dinner. If you miss any of those meals at their appointed time, you can go to the kitchen and get something. The chef is here until seven o'clock, then you're on your own. Across this hall is my father's and stepmother's suite. There's a bathroom next to their room. Downstairs—" she started, but I cut her off.

"Wait, your father is married? Why is this the first time I'm hearing this? I've never seen or heard you mention this."

"I've never had a reason to bring it up. I only told you now because you're going to see her tonight and I don't want things to be awkward. Now, let's continue. Behind that door is stairs that leads down to the basement. There's a rec area, bathroom, and laundry room down there with two guest rooms."

Once she finished showing me the lower level of the house, she led me up a spiral staircase. There were portraits of Kenzie, Tez, Lauren, the twins, Kenna, Kenzie's father, and I'm assuming stepmother lined up against the wall.

"Those double doors right there lead to the east wing. Do not open them, that is Lauren's and Martez's living quarters. This door right here is a bathroom. Now this way is the west wing and this is my living quarters. The only people that walk through those doors without knocking is family. Any of the help will ring the intercom. I rarely lock the door unless I have company because I leave my room door open and the kids' room. The first door right here is the twins' room. The one next to it is my room, and the one across there is a gym. There's a bathroom in both of the bedrooms over here."

I was in awe as I explored McKenzie's living quarters. Her shit was decked out. They went all out for the twins' room and even hers. Instead of having traditional furniture in the sitting area up here, it was set up like a movie theater with reclining seats that fit two people in them. There was a bar and concession stand filled with snacks.

Kenzie is better than me, because I wouldn't be able to spare my mother's feelings if I had the chance to live like this. She'd just have to understand that I deserved the best in life and that I was staying with my father. Then again, looking at this crib, the cars in the driveway, and the security, I'm sure Kenzie's family is doing a lot more than legal business. This looks like they're on some godfather kingpin shit. I kinda want to ask Kenzie about it, but I'm sure she wouldn't tell me if that was the case since she hadn't told me all this time yet.

Both of the twins had fallen asleep, so I went in the bedroom and laid them down then went to the bathroom. By the time I walked back in the front, Blaze walking through the door and over to Kenzie.

"Tamika and Carl just left. Marquis and Makayla are outside playing with McKenna. My body is starting to ache, so I need to go lay down for a minute. Wake me up around five thirty so I can get ready for the dinner."

"Okay, I'll be in there in a couple minutes to check on you," McKenzie replied.

These motherfuckers are in here talking like I'm not standing right here.

"What the fuck is going on? Are you two back together or something?" I finally asked.

"Can you give me a minute to talk to him then I'll be in there?" Kenzie requested.

Blaze nodded before giving me one final look, then walked into McKenzie's room. I noticed he didn't close the door, so I knew he was probably listening in on what we were talking about, and I was about to make sure he got an earful.

"Are going to fucking answer me!" I yelled a little more aggressively than I intended.

"Motherfucker, pipe down yelling at me. You don't get to come here questioning me. The answer to your question is yes, me and Malakai are back together."

"Since when? Because you were just fucking and sucking me damn near every day up until last month. Was this part of your plan then? Fuck me until he resurfaced from wherever the hell he was. Is he the reason you came out here so early?"

"I see your ass trying to be funny but don't worry, because I'll never come close to your dirty dick ass again. I was open and honest with you both times that we were together and both times, you were the one that fucked up. You were the one that didn't trust what we had enough to be honest with me, so don't try and turn this shit around on me. When I chose to get back with you, I wasn't in contact with Malakai at all. Last week was the first time I've seen him in person in almost eight months."

"Well damn, you ain't even let my nut dry before jumping on another dick. What happened to needing time to think?"

"So you telling me you ain't fucked nobody else since we left Memphis?" she countered.

"That's not the point. I'm a man and you're a woman with kids. Your standards are supposed to be higher than mine. You have a daughter and you need to be an example for her. You can jump on whatever dick you want, but I don't want it around my kids. I'm the only father figure they need in their life."

"Go to hell and kick rocks. I can do whatever the fuck I want to do when it comes to my kids. As long as they're safe and in good hands, you have no say so in the situation," McKenzie snapped before walking away.

I might have gone a little too far, but I was fucking pissed. Here I am thinking Kenzie is working on herself or whatever the fuck females do after a break-up to heal, and she's out here living her best life with that nigga Blaze. On top of that, they're sleeping together in a room next me. I was finally seeing how McKenzie felt when she had to share that house with Diane. This is some straight bullshit.

I was left in the living area by myself, so I decided to go in the twins' room and chill. I looked through my suitcase to find something to wear tonight since I only threw on a pair of jogging pants and t-shirt for the flight. After that, I went back in the front and searched for a movie to watch. I could hear McKenzie and Blaze talking, but I couldn't make out what they were saying. I didn't care anyway, so I tuned them out. The door was open so that meant they weren't fucking, and that was plus in my book. I don't know how I would react or feel if I heard them. I shook my head to the idea and went back to searching her catalog for something to watch.

CHAPTER SIXTEEN
BLAZE

I was in the bed trying my best to go to sleep and not listen in on McKenzie's conversation with Chase because it was personal. I trusted her, so I wasn't worried about her trying to be on some slick shit with him, especially with me in the other room. Chase was on some lame shit though. He wanted to make sure I heard their conversation. I guess he thought if I knew he and Kenzie was fucking while I was away I'd push brakes on what we got. Even if she didn't tell me that they were fucking, I still would have pursued her. They could've been fucking up until the day I got out here and it wouldn't have changed a thing.

It was taking everything in me not to go out there and knock him in his shit for the way he was talking to Kenzie, but she was standing her ground. I didn't want to run out there like she was some damsel in distress, because she didn't like that. I kept my cool until I heard him mention not wanting me around the twins. Right there is where the gloves come off. I don't play when it come to my kids or hers. I do just as much for them as he does, and I was there for her throughout the entire pregnancy.

I didn't even have to get up and say anything to Chase about it because McKenzie instantly checked his ass for that shit, making me proud.

McKenzie walked in the room and laid on top of me, burying her face in my chest.

"Are you okay, baby?" I asked her.

"Yeah, I'm fine, he just irks my nerves thinking he has a right to dictate what I do. I don't care what he says, though, you'll always have a place in my kids' life, even it doesn't work for us."

"Don't think like that, it's going to work between us. By this time next year, you're going to have my ring on your finger. We're going to continue to be open and honest with each other, and we won't have anything to worry about. We both might make mistakes down the line, but we'll always be able to fix them together," I reassured her.

"Yeah, you're right, I'm just being practical right now," she stated.

I know I fucked up McKenzie's trust by leaving her, and that's something I will work on every day to gain back because without trust, she won't fully open up and commit to me. Yeah, she says she forgives me and that we can work on us, but I know she's holding back. I can tell from the way she talks and acts with me. We kiss and cuddle together, but that's about it. She hasn't allowed me to touch her sexually since the morning of the bachelor/bachelorette party. We still shower together if we're both up together in the morning or before bed.

I've spent a lot of time with Kenzie since I've been here, but I've been working with Tez while I'm out here. Kenzie told me she's staying until the day after New Year's, so I'm staying until then as well.

I started looking for a house for Tasia, only for her ass to tell me she wanted another apartment. She said a house was too much work and effort. You'd think her grown ass would want something that she can call her own, but I wasn't going to fight her on it as long as she allowed me to pick the area. I was not letting her move back in the hood with my daughter. I'll fight for full custody before that happens.

Josh checked out some apartments in Berwyn since she still wanted to be close to the city. I was cool with that because it wasn't a bad area. I advised her to watch the company she keeps and find a legit job instead trying to hustle out her crib. I'm willing to pay her rent and utilities, but she was in charge of everything else. I already pay for my daughter's daycare and all her health expenses. The only reason I was doing that much was because I'm not on child support. If my daughter needs anything, Tasia lets me know because I don't put money in her hands. She'll use that to get her hair and shit done. I'm not her man, so she won't get that luxury from me.

"Kenz?"

"Hmm," she hummed.

"I'm ready to have the conversation you've been putting off for the past week. If you don't talk to me, I don't know what I can do to fix it."

Kenzie sat up where now her body was straddling my torso.

"You want to know why I don't want to have sex with you?"

"Yes, I mean, I'm willing to wait for as long as you want, but I also want to know the real reason we are waiting. I know you said we have things to work through and we've been doing that on the communication side, but we also have things to work through on the physical side. I get the no sex part, but you barely let me touch you in any sexual way. Last week we were moving a step forward in that direction and now you've completely iced me out. If you don't want a relationship right now, I need you to just let me know and I'll fall back."

McKenzie sat there looking at me for what felt like an eternity until tears started falling from her eyes. I sat up and slid back with my back facing the headboard and held her while she cried in my arms. I have no idea why she's crying, so I don't say anything, but I hold her securely in my arm.

A couple minutes go by and it seems like she calmed down, so I grab some Kleenex from her nightstand and hand it to her.

"That's the problem right there, Kai, I don't want you to fall back. You don't know how bad I need you to make love to me then fuck me all over this bedroom and shower. I've yearned for you the moment I laid eyes on you in the yard that day. It took all of my self-control not to take off my clothes that day and you let you fuck me any way you want. It's like every morning I psych my mind and say today is the day I'm going to let my guard down and give into temptation, but then there's a little voice in the back of my head reminding me that the last time we had sex, you left me. I'm not saying you were only with me for that. It's just I can't get over that part," she explained.

I sighed then leaned over and kissed her forehead. I had done more damage than I realized.

"I will apologize to you every morning if I have to. I know it looked bad, but I never want you to think that I was only out for sex or that I didn't enjoy it. If I could have waited even an extra day, I would have stayed with you. I would have given you a proper goodbye and made love to you from sunup to sundown just so I could savor the feeling. Somebody had literally shot up Tasia's house, burned down one of my traps here, and they did the same to two other ones in Cali. All of our safety was on the line. My brother had to move his wife and kids out here to a safe house. You had just had the twins, so you couldn't drag them all over the world and I wouldn't want you to do that. That's not the life for them, and as long as I was around, y'all were in danger. Do I regret my decision to leave? Of course, I do, but if it meant your life or the twins over mine, I would do it again because there's no way I would be able to live with myself if something happened to y'all, especially because of me."

"I know you did what you had to do, and I love you for that. Just know I want you as bad as you want me. I want to be able to have sex with my man whenever and wherever I want. Be patient with me is all I can ask."

"I can be patient, I just needed to know the reason so I can see if there was anything I can do to comfort you or make things right."

"No, continue doing what you're doing now and everything is all good."

I lifted Kenzie up some so I can lay on my back. She tossed half of her body over mine and we laid there in a comfortable silence. I was sleepy, but there was something I needed to handle before I went to sleep. I also needed to think about what I could do to assure her that I'm not leaving again. I don't want her to end up with abandonment issues because of me.

I laid there for about twenty minutes making sure Kenzie was all the way sleep before I slipped out of the bed. I walked out of the bedroom and Chase was sitting down watching some movie. He was just the person I was looking for. I walked around and stood in front of him, not giving a fuck that I was interrupting his movie.

"Yo, we need to talk about that bullshit ass conversation you and Kenzie had earlier," I said.

"You want to do this right here, right now?" he countered.

"Yeah, because we're stuck under the same roof for the

next week and in each other's lives, so we need some common ground."

"Okay, what do you want to know?"

"I don't want to know shit. I want you to fall back and cut Kenzie some slack. Don't try and make her feel bad because you was on some fuck nigga shit. She gave you two chances and you fumbled both times."

"Man, gone somewhere with that shit because you don't know half the story," he tried to tell me.

"Oh, but I do. You thought you was doing something by saying how she was fucking and sucking you while I was gone, but you weren't. You weren't saying shit that I didn't already know. McKenzie had already told me everything up until the part where she had to fight her stepsister because you hid that you fucked her. You see, McKenzie and I communicate and are honest about everything, which is why I'm the man for her."

"If you're the man for her, how the hell do you up and disappear on her out of nowhere and then come back like nothing happened?"

"That right there is none of your business. McKenzie knows everything, though, so if she didn't tell you, that meant she didn't want you to know. Also, as for you not wanting me around the twins, you might as well dead that situation. I mean, what the fuck did you think was going to happen when you have a woman as bad as Kenzie for a baby mama? You had to know that somebody would be willing to play step-daddy to those kids. Just be glad that it's me, because I can guarantee you they're set for life and they'll always be loved by me. After everything you put her through, you owe her the chance to be happy. I can never take your place. There's a lot of kids that grow up without a father, so yours are already blessed to have two," I told him before walking away and going back in McKenzie's room. I closed the door and laid in bed, leaving him with something to think about.

Had the circumstances been different, I would have knocked his ass in his jaw, but I didn't want to disrespect Kenzie or her family's home. At the end of the day, he's her baby daddy and I put myself in his shoes. If I was in love with my baby mama too, it would be hard for me to accept her moving on. I was never in love with Tamika or Tasia, so I never had to go through this when they were with other men. As long as my kids was cool and in a safe environment, I was good.

I laid in bed, finally falling asleep, when my phone started ringing. I looked down at it and saw that it was Tasia calling me on FaceTime. I didn't want to wake Kenzie but at the same time, if I didn't answer she'd just keep calling. If I stepped away to answer, it'll seem like I'm hiding something, so fuck it.

"What's up, Tasia?" I answered.

"Don't what's up me. Why do I get back here and find out Tamika is the one that picked Kayla up?"

"I had Tamika grab her because she's closer to y'all area than me and she was already on her way out here to drop my son off. I had to help set up and do stuff for this rehearsal dinner."

"So you're coming to stay here tonight afterward?"

McKenzie sat up and looked at me after Tasia asked that question. She gave me a look like she dared me to say the wrong thing.

"Why would I come stay there? All the rooms are full and I'm not about to sleep on no damn couch. I'm staying where I've been staying when I come out here, at McKenzie's family house."

"Wait, and she's staying there too?"

"Where the hell else would she be staying if it's her house too?"

"Bring me my daughter back now. You was supposed to be getting her for a wedding and we all spend Christmas together as a family. Not playing house with that bitch and her family."

I was about to go in on her, but Kenzie interrupted me.

"I'm going to leave and let you finish this conversation in private," McKenzie said.

"You don't have to leave."

"Yes, I do, because I will forget that's Kayla's mama and go beat the shit out of her. I need to go check on the kids anyway and see if everything is almost ready for the dinner."

"Okay, give me a kiss," I told her.

Kenzie leaned over and kissed me sloppily, and I made sure Tasia's disrespectful ass saw it while she was yelling my name in the phone. Once Kenzie was out of the room, I resumed my conversation with Tasia.

"Stop all that fucking yelling. Makayla is staying here with me until Christmas afternoon as planned. We'll be there by two and I'll stay there for Christmas dinner, then I'm coming back to Kenzie's house with Kayla and I'll keep here until New Year's Eve. On the second, we'll all be on a plane together going back to Chicago."

"Okay, bet," Tasia said before hanging up.

Tasia likes to talk crazy, but she never does anything but run her mouth so I'm not worried about her.

I put my phone on DND and then tried to take the nap I was supposed to take an hour ago.

CHAPTER SEVENTEEN
MCKENZIE

This past week flew by faster than I wanted it to. I was enjoying spending time with my family for the holiday. I always feel some type of way when it's almost time for me to leave. Sometimes I wish I could drop everything and move here.

There was tension the day of the rehearsal dinner between Chase and Malakai, but it didn't last. By the next morning, everyone was speaking and discussing their upcoming plans. I was happy about that because I needed Chase and Malakai to get along. I didn't want to have to have separate birthday parties and split holidays with my kids. I wanted them to grow up and see their parents have a healthy coparent relationship. Plus, my brother and father weren't with the bullshit, so we all came to an understanding.

Lauren and Martez's wedding was absolutely beautiful. It was everything that Lauren could imagine, and I was happy they were able to get that. If anyone deserved to be happy, it was them two because Lauren has been by my brother's side forever, even when she shouldn't have.

Martez has always been the best big brother to me and father figure when my father isn't around, but he can be a real asshole sometimes. I used to wonder how Lauren used to put up with his ass, but then I grew up and met Chase. I realized how love will make you do some crazy shit that you normally wouldn't do with a sane mind.

Watching Lauren and Martez get married had me thinking about the possibility of getting married for real someday. I know Malakai is always talking about us getting married, but I've never shared his enthusiasm. Don't get me wrong now, because I would love to get married and have another child with my husband. I just haven't put much thought into the planning part. Most females have an idea of where they want to get married, the location, and a color scheme, but that has never been me.

Martez and Lauren went to Greece for five days for their honeymoon and came back yesterday so we can all bring in New Year's together. Instead of doing it at home, my brother wanted us to bring it in at the strip club he and Don owned. I've never been to a strip blub before, so I'm curious how it will be. My father was having a fit when he found out I was going, but Martez assured him he would keep an eye on me.

"Come on, baby, why are you not ready yet?" Malakai asked as he walked in the room looking sexy as hell. He was rocking some black Versace jeans, a black Versace fitted shirt with the letters in gold, and a pair of black Versace chain reaction sneakers. He finished the look with a gold Cuban-link chain, diamonds in his ear, and a diamond Patek on his wrist. My baby looked and smelled like money.

Typically, Malakai and I would get ready together when we go out, but I needed to do my hair and makeup, so he got dressed and took all the kids to my aunt Victoria's house to give me a little more time. I hurriedly sprayed my Versace

Crystal Bright perfume on before slipping on my clothes. I turned around in the mirror to check myself out. I have on a short black Versace skirt with a gold and black bralette that left little to the imagination. I already know my brother is going to have a fit when he sees what I have on. I grabbed my black Versace heel sandals and put them on along with my gold accessories.

"You look sexy as hell, ma. You definitely staying by my side tonight or I might have to catch a case."

"Touché," I told him before grabbing my clutch and phone. We left the room and headed downstairs where everyone was already waiting for us.

"Girl, you made us wait all that damn time and you half naked. Where the hell is the rest of your clothes, McKenzie?" Martez fussed.

"There's nothing wrong with what I have on. My man thinks I look good and he bought it," I said.

"Man, why the hell would you buy her some shit like that to wear outside?" Martez asked Blaze.

"Technically, all I did was pay for it. I didn't pick it out for her. I gave her my card and told her to buy us something for New Year's. I didn't know what I was wearing until last night and she never showed me what she was wearing. She's good, though, I already told her ass she's staying glued to my hip tonight."

"Leave my sister alone, she looks good as hell. You lucky I don't have a body like hers or I'll be walking around half naked too," Lauren added.

Lauren is a beautiful mixed girl on the thick side. She's half Dominican and Black like us. She's 5'6 with brown eyes, long hair, and weighs about two hundred pounds. She has a nice size ass with big breasts and a pudgy stomach. She could pull off wearing half shirts, but she's not going to have her stomach completely out, even though I think she looks fine with them on.

"No you won't because you know I'll tap that ass," Martez joked.

"Boy bye, you ain't gone do nothing," she challenged, and she hurriedly tried to get away from him.

"Is Papa here or he left already?" I asked.

"He and Isabella are gone to Aunt Victoria's house already."

"Okay, well let's go get this party started," I said.

We all walked out of the house and climbed into the Mercedes-Benz Sprinter. We were riding in one of those because there was a group of us going. It was me, Malakai, Chase, Lauren, Martez, Don, Tyesha, Drea, and two of Martez's workers. Mason and his wife Myra were going as well, but they were going to meet us since the house they were staying at is close to the club.

Once we made it to Skybar, the club was crowded and in full swing. We headed over to our VIP section and before we could sit down, there were waitresses heading our way. The guys ordered some of everything, and I sat back in my seat because I wasn't paying for shit. They all know what I drink so I don't have anything to worry about.

As the waitresses were bringing our drinks, more people were entering our section. Mostly Martez's workers and some groupies they found in the club. Bitches flocked to them niggas like flies on shit just because they have money. Some of them have fucked up personalities and they not all that good looking.

Malakai picked up a bottle of Patrón he ordered and handed it to me.

Everyone was having a good time and vibing to the music. I was tossing shots back like water as the strippers entered our area shaking their asses. The liquor had me feeling nice and lovely. I was enjoying the show until some bitch came over and tried to get Malakai's attention and was damn near sitting on my lap.

"What the fuck, you do see me siting right here, right?"

"My bad, I was just trying to talk to him."

"Well don't, can't you see he's not paying attention to you? So move around," I told her, giving her the shoo signal with my hand.

The girl was about to say something else, but Don stopped her.

"Kira, you heard her, get the fuck from over there," he ordered. I don't know what ties he has with her, but he didn't have to tell her twice.

"You can get a dance if you want," I whispered in Malakai's ear.

"You're offering?" he whispered back.

The liquor courage had me feeling myself, so I pulled him from his seat and walked him toward the back wall away from where everyone was sitting. Some people could still see us, but Martez's back was facing us and I wasn't comfortable giving him a lap dance where my brother could see me. I pushed him against the wall and began grinding on him slowly to the music. I closed my eyes because I was really feeling myself and imagining riding his dick. Malakai's hand grazed my upper thigh and it sent chills down my spine.

I opened my eyes and noticed Chase's eyes glued on me but for the life of me, I couldn't understand why. He had one stripper giving him a lap dance and some other chick whispering in his ear. I hope he didn't think it was fazing me, because he could fuck whomever he wanted. I meant it when I said I'll never touch him again.

The song ended and I was about to sit down, until I heard that it was "Ride or Die" by Megan Thee Stallion.

I'ma ride that dick like a stolen car
I got the best pussy that you had thus far
Which bitch you know goin' hard as me?
I'ma ride or die and I'on need the keys (fuck it up)
I'm finna bounce that ass and drop that ass and pop it like a
shootout
I pulled them panties down, he smilin' like they bought the food out
I hop up on that face and make my hips go like a luau (ahh)
I showed you I'ma gangster, now I wanna see what you 'bout (fuck
it up)

Malakai held my waist as I bounced my ass up and down. I bent over and started twerking my ass on him. I placed my hands on my knees as I continued to throw my ass in a circle. I could feel Malakai's manhood growing on my ass, but that didn't stop me from grinding on him.

Malakai removed one of his hands from my waist and slid it up under my skirt, cupping my pussy. I have on a thong today, so it wasn't hard for him to get to my clit. He rubbed it to the same speed that I was dancing. I held onto his wrist because I was on the verge of cumming. He smacked my hand away and continued playing in my pussy until I was busting in his hand. He grabbed a wet nap from the table next to us and cleaned his hand then wiped me clean with a dry napkin.

I turned around and wrapped my arms around his neck, kissing him sloppily.

"If you trying to get fucked in the club, just say that." He smirked.

"No, I'm not, but I want to when we get home. I want to feel all of you tonight in every hole," I told him seductively.

"Girl, you better stop talking like that before I have the driver take us back home before they drop the ball," he said seriously.

"Come with me so I can freshen up."

"Okay, I can go wash my hands too."

We walked from our section and Lauren stopped us to see where we were going. When I told her the bathroom, she volunteered to go with me. We all left the section and as we were heading to the bathroom, we saw Tasia and Kim dancing on each other by the bar. I guess they're still a thing without Malakai being involved. I was hoping that they didn't see us, but there was no such luck. Before we could even make to the line, they came rushing over to us.

Malakai immediately pulled me close to him when he saw them coming my way.

"So that's what we on now, Blaze? You have us come out here for the holidays, but we only see you on Christmas. You sent an invite to Myra and Mason to come here, but you forgot all about us," Kim said loudly.

"I didn't forget about y'all. I didn't send you two an invite because I had no intention on bringing in the new year with either of you. I told you all that we could spend Christmas together and that's what I did. I left it up to you to find your own New Year's plans," Malakai replied.

"Man, this whole situation is fucked up and you know it. What we had going on was good and you ruined it all for this young ass girl. We were the ones feeding, cleaning, and nursing you back to health. Does she know that while you were away you were fucking both of us for the last few months?"

"Yeah, I knew, and thank you for taking care of him while he was away, but he's back now and I got it from here. You know y'all quick to keep calling me a lil' ass girl when y'all talking to him, but that don't stop him from sucking on my pussy or me twirling on his dick. Find somebody else for y'all weird ass threesome, because this one right here will have no parts in it," I pointed out.

Kim and Tasia were in a state of shock when I mentioned him sucking on my pussy because he doesn't give either of them head. I'm not sure if he ever did before or not since neither of them was ever his girlfriend.

"If y'all don't get the fuck on somewhere trying to start some shit, I will embarrass y'all. What the fuck y'all doing all this for? Don't try to act like I'm sneaking behind y'all back or shit. You both know that I'm back with McKenzie, and she knows everything that went on between us while we were gone. I told you in the beginning that what we had wouldn't last. I appreciate everything you two did to help me, but I didn't ask you to. Mason hired people to do what you were doing. You wanted to help, so I allowed it. When I left Cali, I told y'all I was done with all that shit. It's not my fault if you didn't believe me," Malakai told them.

"Okay, so what are we doing about going home?" Tasia asked.

"We're leaving on Monday morning as planned. Mason is leaving the same day so he's bringing y'all with him. He's going home and all of us are going to Chicago. When we get there, you'll be moving into your new spot. Josh already got all of your stuff from the storage, so it's ready for you. Kim will get dropped off wherever she wants to go, then me and Kenzie are going to either my house or hers," he explained.

"Okay cool, I'm tired of this shit with you, Blaze. Don't come running to me when you get tired of robbing the cradle," Tasia cried, on the verge of tears, before turning to leave. Kim was right behind her to console her.

I shrugged my shoulders and went to the bathroom. I prayed them bitches got everything out of their system because I was not about to let them ruin my night.

"Don't pay them any attention. They're just mad because they know it's over for them," Lauren said.

"Girl, I'm not worried about them. I'm about freshen up and go finish enjoying the rest of the night with my man." I smiled.

"I know that's right, bitch," she laughed.

Lauren and I finished up in the bathroom, and Malakai was standing there waiting for us. We made our way back to our section and finished knocking back drinks and dancing. It was almost two o'clock when we finally left the club. Everyone wanted to go hang out more at the house, but me and Malakai had other plans that didn't include a crowd.

CHAPTER EIGHTEEN

BLAZE

W e left the club, and we couldn't get back to the house fast enough. Me and Kenzie's hands were all over each other. Luckily, we were in the back row alone so no one could see what we're doing unless they were being nosey. Had we drove on our own, I would have pulled over and broke her off in a parking lot just to get that first nut off. She had me horny ever since that little dance she did for me. She just doesn't know how bad I wanted to lift her skirt up and fuck her right then and there. The only reason I didn't do it is because I haven't had sex with her in all this time, so I wanted our first time to be right. Now any other time, I don't give a fuck. If she pulls some shit like that and she got on a little ass skirt, I'm pulling out my dick and giving her what she is asking for.

When we made it to the house, everyone went out back on the patio to drink and smoke. The cook had left sandwiches, fruit, and chicken for when we made it back. I grabbed a tray and put two champagne flutes on it, a bowl of ice, strawberries, and a plate of food for us to share. I already have a bottle of Moet upstairs at Kenzie's mini bar.

I was about to dip out the kitchen when my brother walked over to me.

"What's up, man, where's Kenzie? Y'all not coming outside to hang out? I know y'all not about to go to bed already," he said.

"Nah, we not coming out, but we not going to bed either. We want to finish bringing in the new year alone," I told him, showing him my tray.

"Ohhhh, I see, do you think it'll be cool with her if me and Myra stay tonight?"

"Yeah, that's cool. When you ready to go to bed, go up the stairs and turn right. When you see the double doors, push them open. Kenzie has linen in the closest and y'all can sleep on one of her seats. They recline all the way out like a bed."

"Okay, thank you."

"You're welcome, don't knock on the bedroom door unless it's important," I warned him.

"Go do you, bro, I'll be good. If I need something, I'll text you."

I went upstairs and grabbed the Moet then headed toward Kenzie's room. I walked inside, closing and locking it just in case someone decided they wanted to bust in the wrong room. I placed the tray on the end table she has in her room. I stripped out of all my clothes and laid them on the pile next to hers before walking into the bathroom.

I walked around to her shower area and she was already in there washing up. I climbed in with her and stood in front since she was almost done. She grabbed a loofah and lathered it with soap before washing my back with it.

"Turn around," she demanded.

I did as she said, and she started cleaning my chest.

Reaching to my dick, she starts lathering and stroking it slowly, causing me to close my eyes. I couldn't take it anymore, I needed to bury myself in her. I looked deeply in her eyes before crashing my lips into hers. Our tongues tangled and she fought for dominance, but I won.

I lifted her by her waist and she instinctively wrapped her legs around me. I put her back up against the wall and slowly pushed my dick inside of her.

"Shittt," I moaned as her pussy wrapped around my dick like a glove. Her shit was dripping wet, and I already knew I wasn't going to last. Moving in and out of her at a steady pace felt so damn good.

"Fuck, that feels good as hell," Kenzie moaned in my ear as she bit down on my earlobe.

I started bouncing her up and down on my dick faster. Her moans and screams were echoing throughout the bathroom, and it was music to my ears. I bit down on her shoulder and her pussy tightened around my dick. She continued do that and had me ready to bust.

"Fuck, Kenzie, I'm about to nut, ma. Cum with me," I groaned as I bit down on her shoulder a little harder to muffle the scream that damn near came out of my mouth. She continued clenching her pussy, causing both of us to cum together. I held her in place for a minute to try and catch my breath. My dick was jumping and ready for more, but I wanted to finish in the bedroom.

I let Kenzie down gently and we finished our shower. We dried off and I carried her back to the bedroom. I gently laid her down on the bed and moisturized her body with some oil. She was glistening from head to toe by the time I was done.

We drank some of the Moet and fed each other strawberries with no words exchanged. Her lust-filled eyes stayed locked on mine, like she was imagining the things she wanted to do to me.

"Tell me what's on your mind, baby. I'm at your disposal," I told her.

"I want to ride your face until I cum all in your goatee," McKenzie purred in my ear.

I swallowed the strawberry that was in my mouth and washed it down with the last of my Moet then laid back on the bed. She wasted no time sitting on my face. She immediately started moaning as my tongue entered her folds. She held on to her headboard and wound her hips in a circular motion. I was slurping, licking, and sucking all on her shit. Her sweet nectar was taking me into overdrive.

McKenzie picked up the pace and I could tell she was close to cumming. She was squirming and moving all over the place. I put a vice grip on her hips and made her take the tongue lashing I was giving her.

"Fuccckkk, I'm cummming," she cried out as she squirted all over my face. I had to turn my head some because it felt like she was trying to drown me in the pussy. Her juices were sliding out of my mouth, down to my goatee, and all over my chest.

McKenzie climbed off of my face and straddled my chest backward as she gripped my dick in her hands. She spit on it then licked the precum before placing it in her mouth. That's what the fuck I'm talking about. I don't even have to ask her to give me some head.

"God damn," I mumbled as she started doing her thing. There was no need for me to move an inch because she knew exactly what she was doing. All I saw was her ass in my face and she bobbed up and down on my dick.

I reached out and I rubbed my hand across her pussy to wet it. I used my index finger and slid it inside of her ass, causing her to hum on my dick. I pushed my finger in and out of her, and that caused her to suck my dick harder. My legs started shaking as I nutted in her mouth. I removed my finger from her ass as she turned around and slid down on my dick. I leaned up some and put one of her titties in my mouth as she bounced up and down on my dick. She only lasted about five minutes until she was cumming again.

I flipped her over on her back and slid inside of her gently. I leaned over and kissed her gently as I stroked her slowly.

"I missed the shit out of you, Kenzie. I missed you being mine and our friendship. I love you so fucking much," I told her as I gave her deep, slow strokes, making sure to hit her spot every time."

"Ohhhh, I missed us to, babbyyy," she moaned out.

I continued whispering how much I loved and missed her, all of my future plans for us, until she was cumming all over my dick. Tears were falling from her eyes as I continued to make love to her. Every time one dropped, I kissed it away. We made love for another forty minutes until I was nutting all in her. I hope her birth control is as strong as it's supposed to be. If not, after tonight, were about to have another mini me in this world nine months from now.

"Get up, let's go shower before you fall asleep," I told her.

"You don't have to worry about me falling asleep. I just hope you have enough energy to keep up with me tonight."

"Shittt, I was trying to give you a break. I can go all night," I told her seriously.

Kenzie had the kind of pussy that made me want to live in it. Like I could make love to her for breakfast, lunch, and dinner. The last time I fucked all night was the first time we had sex. The most Kim and Tasia were getting from me was a couple rounds that lasted about an hour. I was never putting my all into fucking them. My dick just that good that it gets bitches hooked from the first stroke.

Kenzie and I went in her bathroom and took a quick shower then went back to the bedroom and picked up where we left off. She wasn't playing when she said she wanted to go all night. We took a couple breaks in between, but her little ass was wearing me out. I guess you can say we were making up for lost time. I know my brother, Mason, Myra and Chase got an earful, because McKenzie didn't make an attempt to be quiet at all.

I'm just glad that her father and brother's rooms are nowhere near hers or they'd think I was in here trying to murder her when the only thing I wanted to murder was the pussy. It wasn't until the sun started coming out three hours later that she was ready to tap out.

"Malakai," Kenzie called my name as she laid on my chest.

"Huh," I asked, half asleep.

"I love you too, and I want it to always be like this for us."

I pulled her closer to me and kissed her forehead. It was only a matter of minutes until she was out, and I was right behind her.

The following day, I woke up to someone knocking on the bedroom door. I groaned and looked over at the clock and saw it was already 12:35 p.m. McKenzie has solid thermal black-out curtains up at her window, and she made sure to close them all the way before we went to sleep last night. She was knocked out and her naked body was thrown across me. I pulled the covers over her before saying who is it.

"It's me, are y'all decent enough for me to come in?" Tez asked.

"Yeah," I called out.

Tez opened the door and walked in.

"My pops told me to come check on y'all since you two

didn't come down for breakfast or lunch. I told him y'all was good, but he said to come up here anyway and tell y'all to get up. It's the last day y'all here so he wants to have a family barbecue. He invited your brother and his wife. I'm about to go get the kids now."

"Okay, we'll be down in about an hour."

"Nah, my nigga, get her up now and get dressed. Y'all don't have time for all that extra shit either," he said before walking out of the room.

I shook McKenzie slightly and she stirred in my arms then rolled over. I had worn her little ass out last night. If her pussy wasn't swollen, I would have woken her up with some dick.

I climbed out of bed and took a piss then filled her tub up with hot water. I added a bath bomb and some bubbles to it then turned on the jets. I left the bathroom and Kenzie was still half way asleep.

"Baby, wake up, your dad is at the door," I told her.

She instantly jumped out of bed and wrapped the sheet around her. She was scrambling looking for something to throw on. You'd think she was a teenager whose parents came home early and were about to catch her fucking.

"Why the hell aren't you getting dressed?" she whisper yelled.

"I'm kidding, he did send Tez up here to check on you though. I ran you a bath, so come on so you can soak."

"I can't walk, pick me up," she whined.

I picked her up and she wrapped her legs around me. She placed her lips on mine and we kissed until we made it to the bathtub. I got in first then she got in with me. I massaged her shoulders and we chilled in the tub. She threw her head back and laid on my chest. We sat there for about five minutes in a comfortable silence.

"Before we settle completely down and get married, I want

to try a threesome," she blurted out, shocking the hell out of me.

"What? Are you serious?"

"Yeah, I've always been curious what it was like. I'd like to get everything out of my system before we get married so there's no mishaps."

"Okay, I'll surprise you one day."

We finished our bath and got out. I cleaned the tub while she brushed her teeth and combed her hair. Once she was done, she dried off. I put on a pair of basketball shorts and a tank top since we were just hanging around the house. She put on a pair of biker shorts with a tank top and hoody. That hoody was about to draw so much attention, but she had hickeys on her neck, shoulder, and breasts. I wasn't even sucking on her that hard, so I didn't expect that.

We went downstairs to the family room. Victor, Isabella, Lauren, and Chase were sitting down watching TV.

We spoke to everyone and Kenzie hugged her father.

"McKenzie, are you cold? I can have Abigail adjust the temperature," Isabella said with her thick accent.

"No, I'm fine. It can stay how it is."

McKenzie and I sat down on the couch next to Lauren.

"You should've put on pants too if you we're trying to hide marks," Lauren said lowly so only me and Kenzie could hear.

Kenzie looked at Lauren confused then looked down at her thighs. There were a couple small hickeys and partial fingerprints on her legs. Kenzie's face turned bright red.

"Relax, baby, it's not that bad," I told Kenzie.

"Shit, it ain't no better for you. You got hickeys on your neck too. Y'all should've stayed down here and ate last night if y'all was that hungry," Lauren joked.

"Shut up before Papa hears you," McKenzie replied.

"He not blind, that's why he looking at Malakai like he want to use him for target practice."

I looked over at Victor, and he was definitely staring at me like he knew I slutted his baby girl out last night.

"Papa, what day are you coming to Chicago?" McKenzie asked, trying to get her father's attention away from me.

"We'll be there on the fifteenth and staying for a week, so we'll be there for their birthday and party. Do you have everything you need for it? I told you to tell me how much it costs and I'll send you money."

"I told you we have everything covered. Chase gave me money toward it and Malakai paid for the rest. All y'all have to do is show up," McKenzie replied.

Chase said something under his breath after hearing that. All I know is he better not say anything to Kenzie about me helping pay for the party. He should be happy his kids got somebody that's willing to be there financially as well and not just trying to fuck on their mama.

The twins' birthday is in two weeks and McKenzie rented out a spot to throw a party. She ordered a jumpy house and different concession stands along with custom-made decorations. Even though we weren't talking at the time, I still wanted to help pay for their party so I sent money, not knowing how much it'll cost, but I wanted her to be able to get whatever she wanted without a budget.

"Blaze, come, let me talk to you for a minute," Victor said.

I looked at McKenzie then got up from the couch and followed him to his office. He closed the door behind us and got right to the point.

"Now that you are back in my daughter's life, what are your intentions? I only ask this because she was a wreck when you first left, but I vouched for you and told her that she should sit down and listen to you. I need to know that you don't want her to play games or just for sex."

"Sir, I love your daughter and I have no intentions on playing games with her. I want to continue to build her trust with me and when the time is right, ask her to be my wife. I want to take care of her and the kids. I know that it's a package deal and I'm going to stick around. By the time she has a child by me, I intend to be out of the game or at least to the point where I don't have to touch drugs," I told him honestly.

Victor nodded his head in approval.

"Good, because I can't stand that motherfucker she has her kids by, but I tolerate him for the sake of them. I know that you to will have ups and downs, and I won't get involved in your business, but the moment my baby comes crying on my shoulder because of you, we're going to have a problem."

"I understand, but you don't have to worry about that," I assured him.

Victor and I sat and talked for a few more minutes before we went back to join everyone in the living room.

CHAPTER NINETEEN

MCKENZIE

Malakai and I have been back together officially a month now, and let's just say that we're still in the honeymoon phase. We make love almost every day and we haven't spent a night apart. We alternate between his house and mine. We go on little outings with the twins and when he's not working, he's at home helping me get the kids ready for bed. He makes sure that the needs of me and the kids are met before he goes out and hits the streets. I make sure that he has a home-cooked meal every night that he comes home.

"When do you think the right time is for us to get married?" Malakai asked out of nowhere. We had just finished showering and had a hot, steamy sex session, and now I was laying in his arms halfway asleep. Every night before we go to bed, we lay in each other's arms and discuss how our day went or what we want for our future.

"Uhm, I don't know. I guess it depends on when you propose to me."

"Baby, if I thought you'd say yes right now, I'd get up in the morning and get you a fat ass rock," he replied.

I chuckled slightly because I knew he was serious. He's been trying to convince me to move in with him since we got back in Chicago. I told him that I needed a little more time before we took that step. Chase was the only guy I lived with and that was for a few months. I don't even know if that counts because we didn't officially live together. He had two drawers here with clothes and toiletries. He had no mementos or personal items here.

Once you move in with someone that's an entirely different commitment. You have to figure out whose furniture is going to stay and whose is going to go. No one thing is ever yours again. At least now if Malakai was to piss me off, I can get up and go home or send him home. If we live together, we will have to work on things like adults because there's nowhere to run. I'll be damn if I accept him getting mad and he goes somewhere else to sleep while we live together, and low and behold, don't let the streetlights beat you home.

"Okay, so, I've been thinking about this move in thing. How would it work as far as Chase seeing the kids?"

"He would come here and see them. You can keep the same arrangement here that you already have. He can come and spend time with them, but he has to be gone by the time they go to sleep. He needs to call before he shows up. I'll never stop him from coming here to see them unless it's past nine, then he has no reason to be knocking on our door because they will be in bed already."

"Okay, let's make a deal. I will gradually start moving in here and any time after my twenty-first birthday, you can propose without worrying about me freezing up or saying no."

Tori had already started moving out of the house because she was moving in with her boyfriend, so it was time for me to finally put my big girl panties on. I needed to stop overthinking and just go with the flow of things in my life. I can't keep holding back with a man that's willing to give me his all. He ready to give me the world and I need to allow him.

I closed my eyes and finally fell asleep, only to be awakened thirty minutes later to the sound of a ringing phone. I looked over at the clock and saw that it was one thirty in the morning.

"Malakai, wake up and get your phone. Who the fuck calling you this time of night?" I asked with a slight attitude.

He grumbled something then reached over to the nightstand and grabbed his phone. He looked down at it then put it back where he got it from.

"That's not my phone it's yours, so who the fuck calling you this time of night?" he asked, flipping the script.

I leaned over him and grabbed my phone. I saw that it was Aniyah and called her right back. I know something is going on because she doesn't call me this time of night.

"Oh my god, McKenzie, I need your help. I think my water just broke and I'm home alone. I tried to call Quan and he's not picking up. I'm so scared and I don't know what to do," she rambled on.

"Stay on the phone with me. I'm going to call an ambulance and meet you at the hospital. Practice your breathing and try to relax," I told her as I climbed out of bed.

I grabbed my Malakai's phone and dialed 911.

"911, what's your emergency?"

"My sister is in labor and she needs an ambulance to 2011 W. Lake Street."

"Alright, we'll send someone right away."

"I hate to ask this, but can you watch the kids for me while I go to the hospital with Aniyah? She's in labor and she's alone since Quan isn't answering his phone."

"Of course, I'll watch them for you. Keep me posted on

what's going on and if you need me, hit my line. Be safe driving out there this time of night. Let me know when you make it."

"I will, thank you, and I love you."

"I love you too," Malakai replied.

I've left the kids alone with Malakai to make a store runs but never for a long period of time. He keeps asking me to give him more responsibilities with them, so I guess tonight will prove if he can handle it.

I threw on a jogging suit and a pair of sneakers before leaving out of the house. I jumped in the car and tried to keep my sister calm until the ambulance showed up. The hospital is five minutes from where she lives and about twenty-five minutes from where I am.

By the time I made it to the hospital, they had already wheeled Aniyah to labor and delivery. I called Quan's phone and he didn't answer. I left him a voicemail letting him know he needed to hurry up and come to the hospital.

If I was Aniyah, when this is over, I'd knock Quan upside his head. Here it is damn near two in the morning and he's not at home or answering his calls. The only time this is excusable is if Malakai is lying in a ditch, hospital, or jail. Other than that, I'm going Katie Kaboom. I don't care how much shit going on in the streets, you better call and let your location be known for reassurance. Times like this make me thankful for having a thoughtful man that puts my thoughts into consideration.

I took the elevator up to the fifth floor and went to the room they told me Aniyah was in. I walked in and sat in a chair by her bed.

"I'm so sorry for waking you up. I just didn't know who else to call. Where are the twins?"

"You don't have to apologize. I told you I'll be here for you. We were at Malakai's house when you called, so he's keeping them."

"Okay, I'm glad you two were able to work things out. At least one of us can be happy," she said, mumbling the last part.

"Aniyah, you don't have to put up with his shit. Tori just moved out so you can move in with me if you want to until you can get on your feet. I'll help you out with the baby if you need me to while you look for a job or finish school. I'm barely there anyway and Malakai wants me to move in with him."

"I wish it was that simple, Kenzie, but it's not. It's not like he's just my boyfriend or baby daddy. He's my husband and we made vows to be together forever."

"Well, where is your husband right now, Aniyah? It's the middle of the night and you're in labor while he's nowhere to be found. He knows it's close to your due date so he should be on standby. Hell, even if you weren't in labor, you should know where he is this time of night."

"He's out handling business, Kenzie. All of us can't have a perfect man like Blaze fall from the sky and into our laps. My man has to get his hands dirty to provide for us."

I was about to go off on her for that little slick ass comment, but I had to remind myself that she's in the hospital and in her feelings because her so-called husband isn't here. We remained quiet for the next three hours to prevent ourselves from saying something we'll regret later. I sat there and mostly text Malakai because he said he couldn't sleep while I was out this time of night.

I told him what was going on and he talked me off the ledge, because I was about to leave and go find Quan's trifling ass, but he reminded me that my sister needs me more. I couldn't believe I was more pissed than Aniyah was for Quan not being here.

I know Chase missed the birth of our twins, but that was Diane's fault. It wasn't because he didn't answer the phone. We weren't even together anymore anyway, and we didn't live together. I at least had Malakai and the rest of my family there. Not to mention, I only went into labor because of a car accident.

Aniyah and I were on good terms, though, so I didn't want to fight with her over her man. If she wanted to be stupid behind him that's on her, but I'll be the good little sister to help her put the pieces back together when they crumble. Baby, when I say they're going to crumble, they are, because no way in hell should it be five in the morning and that nigga ain't returned not one phone call or text message. I know his phone not dead because the message delivered.

"Hey, Mrs. Stevens, it looks like you're six centimeters. We have to wait a little longer before you can push," Dr. Gilmore said.

The doctor came every hour on the hour to check Aniyah's cervix. It was going on 7:30 a.m. when she was fully dilated and ready to push.

"Okay, Aniyah, I need you to push on the count of three," Dr. Gilmore coached her.

I held Aniyah's hand as the doctor counted. She was squeezing the shit out of my hand and she had me ready to cry. I had just took a brace off my hand a couple months ago and she was about to have me putting it back on again.

Aniyah pushed as hard as she could then stopped to catch a break.

"You're doing good, Niyah, the head is coming out," I told her.

"Let's get another big push," the doctor said.

"Arrggggh," Aniyah screamed as she pushed again.

Half of the baby's body came out.

"Come on, one more big push," Dr. Gilmore instructed her.

"I can't do this. I'm tired," Aniyah cried.

"Come on, sis, you can do this. One more push and you'll be able to meet your baby boy."

The doctor counted to three again, and Aniyah pushed as hard as she could until her baby was completely out.

The baby was quiet for a minute, then we heard a high-pitched cry.

"Congratulations, you have a baby boy. Young lady, would you like to cut the umbilical cord?" the doctor asked me.

I took the scissors from the nurse and cut the cord. They took him over to the corner to weigh and measure him before bringing him over to Niyah.

"Here's your bundle of joy. He's 7 lbs, 8 oz, and 21 inches. You can hold him for a minute while we clean you up, then we have to take him away to do an examination."

I watched as my sister held her baby, and my heart melted. I love being a mother to the twins and I can't wait to have another baby. I missed out on this moment when I went into labor. A cesarian was never a part of my plan. I wasn't the first person to see my kids or hear their cries. I wanted to experience everything all over again and the next time around, hopefully it will go as I planned.

They took the baby away and moved Aniyah to a room. I stayed with her until almost eight. That was when Quan came strolling in like he didn't just miss the birth of his baby. I didn't want to be anywhere near him right now.

"Thanks, Kenzie, for being here with her. I got up with some shit and didn't see that y'all was calling me."

"Yeah, I bet," I replied.

"What the hell is that supposed to mean?"

"It means that you were already late so you could have went home and washed your ass already. You smell like some cheap perfume, and unless you and my sister just finished fucking yesterday before she went into labor, that hickey didn't come from her."

"Just mind your own business. You don't know what you're talking about."

"Aniyah might fall for that shit and that's between you two, but don't talk to me like I'm stupid. Your dumb ass is just as bad as Chase. For the life of me, I don't know why you asked her to marry you."

"You're just jealous because she's married and you're not."

"Nigga, please, I'd rather be single than married to a man like you. I'm not desperate for love or attention. If you were my man, I would have been in jail by now for domestic."

Quan was about to respond, but Aniyah woke up and started talking, getting both of our attention.

"Quan, you made it. I thought something happened to you," Aniyah said groggily.

"Hey baby, I'm sorry I missed the baby's birth. I was in the middle of something and my phone was in the car."

"It's okay, I understand. I'm just glad you're okay."

I stood there looking at their interaction, and it was making me sick to the stomach. It had me thinking that it was normal for Quan to come and go as he pleased because Aniyah is a little too calm for my soul. I don't give a fuck if I just had a baby or not, I would have picked up something and knocked his ass upside his head. I couldn't take it anymore. I told Aniyah goodbye and rushed out the room before she could even respond.

I left the hospital and drove straight to Malakai's house. The entire drive was a blur because I was in tunnel vision. There was no way that my big sister could be this god damn stupid. I parked my car in the driveway and used my key to enter Malakai's house.

When I walked in, he was sitting on the couch watching cartoons and the twins were in their play pen.

"Hey baby, why didn't you tell me you were on your way home?"

"I'm sorry, I was pissed and had to get away from that hospital," I said as I walked over and sat on his lap.

"What happened?"

"Quan just showed up at the hospital at 8:00 with hickeys and smelling like cheap perfume. He had already missed the birth of his baby, so the least he could have done was show up presentable. Then Aniyah's so excited to see him that she's missing all the signs. Then again, maybe she didn't miss them but is oblivious to the situation because he does this on the regular. I was so pissed that I didn't even stay to find out the baby's name."

"I know that's your sister, but you can't get involved. You have to give her a chance to figure it out on her own. It's okay for you to offer help to her, but you can't make her accept it."

"You're right but just know if you ever pull some shit like this, especially when I'm in labor, your ass will be in a hospital room of your own."

"Come on now, don't let what happened with them start making you doubt me. We don't even live together, and we're not married, and I never let the sun beat me home. We as men know what we can and can't get away with. I know how you are, so I would never try to play you like that."

"As long as you know." I smirked.

"Are you hungry? I can cook something for you. I made the twins oatmeal so now we're just chilling."

"No, I'm alright. I just need a nap. What time do you have to leave for work?"

"Gone ahead and go to sleep. I can keep an eye on them for

you. I already called Josh and told him I won't be in until later this afternoon."

"Okay, thank you, baby," I told him before heading upstairs to his bedroom. I put my phone on silent because I didn't want to talk to anybody. All I wanted to do was sleep away the headache that was forming.

When I woke up, it was already one o'clock and I was feeling refreshed. I climbed out of bed and walked downstairs to the living room. The twins were napping, and Malakai was sitting down watching a football game.

I sat down on his lap and kissed his lips gently.

"Hey, sleepy head," he said in between kisses.

"What time do you have to leave?" I asked him.

"Today is Sunday, so you know I just go to the warehouse for about two to three hours, then I'll be back. What's up?"

"Nothing, I can wait until you get back."

"Wait for what? You want some dick?" he asked as he leaned over and placed kisses on my neck.

"Yeah, but you already put off going long enough for me, so I'll wait until you get back."

"Baby, let's get something straight. This dick belongs to you, so if I'm here and you want it, all you have to do is sit on it. If you need some head, all you have to do is sit on my face for that too. Hell, if I'm not here, all you have to do is call and tell me you're horny and I'll be on my way, unless I'm in a meeting, then you'll have to wait until that's over. Because you already know when I want some pussy, I'm sliding up in you with no warning," he reminded me as he lifted my shirt over my head.

We had a quickie right there on the couch because we didn't know how long the kids would be sleep. I was never one to be into quickies, but Malakai's quickies were nice because he made sure I came with him within those five or ten minutes.

We only have those during the day. At night, he makes sure to take his time until both of us are thoroughly pleased.

We went upstairs and took a quick shower, then Malakai left to meet Josh. I decided to do some cleaning and start preparing dinner. I was making short ribs, macaroni, greens, and corn bread. I wanted everything to be done by the time Malakai made it home.

Since I was up now, I took my phone off silent and saw that I had a missed call from Tyrese. We were on speaking terms, but I still wasn't close to my brother. I forgave him for the Chase situation, but I still couldn't forgive him for just standing there when that shit went down between me and Ricky at the house. Or even the fact that he allows Ricky to treat my mother the way he does. I wouldn't put it past him to know that Quan and Shavon were fucking. He spends most of his time at the trap and that's where Quan takes her. It wouldn't surprise me if he was staying quiet because she was sucking his dick too.

I dialed Tyrese's number and he answered on the first ring.

"What the fuck did you do to Quan and Aniyah? They were arguing and upset when I went up to the hospital and it had to do with you."

I took the phone off my ear for a minute because I know he wasn't coming at me this way.

"Man, don't fucking call my phone talking to me like I'm one of your bitches. If you want to ask me something and you expect an answer, then I advise you to ask properly."

"I can call and talk however way I want when you're being insensitive while she's in the hospital. If you feel a certain way about Aniyah or Quan, then stay the fuck away from them."

"Oh, you got me all the way fucked up now. I'm so mother-fucking close to forgetting you're my brother and having some-body fuck your bitch ass up. I was the one that she called at two o'clock in the morning to come with her because her dirty dick ass husband wasn't answering the phone. I got out of my bed with my nigga in the middle of the night, leaving my kids to go be with her, only for her to make excuses for that dumb ass nigga who came strolling in at eight in the morning. I didn't say anything else to Aniyah about it, but hell yeah, I said something to Quan about it, even though you should be the one saying something. You're so busy trying to fit in with those niggas that you allow them to dog your sisters out, but fuck that. I don't need none of their asses, so I'm going to speak my mind. I don't know why you hate me so much all of a sudden and frankly, I don't give a fuck anymore. Let this be the last time you call my phone talking crazy, or I'm going to let them goons loose on your ass," I warned him before hanging up.

Martez and Malakai both have been refraining from fucking Tyrese up because he's my brother. Neither of them like the way he treats me, mainly because I've cried to both of them about him. I couldn't understand how your own flesh and blood could hate your guts for no reason. I've never done anything wrong to my brother. I've always been there when he needed or wanted something. I lent him I don't know how much money when I lived at my mother's house, and he never paid me back. I didn't trip on it or ask him for it. It's not my fault that I'm living a better life than them. That has to do with my mother giving up the goods to a rich man that takes care of his responsibility. I'm over Tyrese and Quan though. If I don't ever see or talk to either of their asses again, I'll be a-okay.

CHAPTER TWENTY

QUAN

Aniyah and baby Alex are lying in bed next to me knocked out, but I can't sleep worth shit. My mind has been real heavy lately. I've been thinking about how much I been fucking up all because of Shavon. It's been almost a week since I missed the birth of my son and I still can't believe that shit. I've been by Aniyah's side every day since, chilling with her and my son. I have business to take care of, but I have to make things right at home first.

I'm trying to prove to Aniyah that she doesn't have to do this on her own. She says she understands why I wasn't there, but I know that doesn't stop her from being disappointed. She has every right to be hurt and even curse me out, but she hasn't done it yet. I'd like to think it's because my son is keeping her calm. I love the hell out of him and I know that I have to make some changes in my life because if I keep this shit up, I'm going to lose my family.

Just thinking about that day Aniyah went into labor makes me want to kick my own ass. I had been busy running around all day making moves. I was tired as hell and didn't have the energy to drive home, so I went to Shavon's crib to take a nap since she didn't live far from the trap.

I had set my alarm for me to get up in an hour but when I got there, Shavon wouldn't let me go to sleep without giving her some dick first. Aniyah was pregnant as hell and hadn't been in the mood for sex lately, so I gave her what she wanted and then went to sleep. By the time I woke up, it was 7:30 in the morning. The dumb ass bitch had put my phone in airplane mode. I was mad as hell when I took it out and saw all the text messages and voicemails I had. I could've beat the shit out of her ass, but I had to hurry up and leave to get to the hospital. I was praying during the entire drive that she hadn't gone into labor yet.

When I made it to the hospital and gave them Aniyah's name, they told me she was on the mother-baby unit. I knew right then and there that she had the baby. I was already thinking of a lie during the ride on the elevator. Once I made to the room, the look on Kenzie's face showed me that she was pissed. I didn't expect her to go in on me like she did, but I shouldn't have been surprised because I see the way she was with Chase. She was never one to bite her tongue. I had fucked up and there was no way around it, so I let her talk her shit. I told her that she was just jealous of Aniyah but the truth is, I was the one jealous of Chase. That nigga got to be one dumb motherfucker to mess up with Kenzie. If I was him, the moment Kenzie showed me attention, I would have left Diane in the dust. It was no comparing her to any of the females we used to fuck with.

Back in the day, I had a mad crush on Kenzie but once I got serious with Aniyah, I pushed those feelings to the side because I knew I could never cross that line. I would never hurt Aniyah like that or come between her and her sister's relationship.

I met Kenzie and Aniyah at the same time one day at the park. My eyes were on Kenzie and I wanted her bad. It wasn't about her looks, though, because Aniyah is just as beautiful to me. It was the way she carried herself that drew me into her. She was confident and knew she was the shit. At the time, I was eighteen and she was fifteen, but I didn't care about her age. I was ready to shoot my shot until I saw Chris walk up and kiss her. I didn't want no beef with him over a female, so I didn't approach her. I approached her sister instead.

Aniyah was sixteen with the body of a vixen. She was attractive as hell, but I wasn't looking for a relationship. All I wanted to do was fuck, but she wasn't going. She told me she was a virgin and wanted to wait. I debated on ending things with her ass that same night but deep down, I felt like she was worth it.

I fucked around on Aniyah up until she decided she was ready to sleep with me five months into our relationship. I tried my best to be faithful to her after she gave up her virginity, but I hated that I had to teach her everything. Her pussy was good, but she didn't know how to work it. I was tired of doing all the work, so I didn't put much effort into our sex. I tried to get her to watch porn so she could learn how to suck dick better and eventually, she caught on.

Everything was good between us up until the day she caught me with Shavon at the trap. That was the first time I fucked Shavon and cheated in over a year. I don't know what made me do the shit knowing that was Aniyah's stepsister. I was high as hell chilling in the back room when Shavon came in locking the door. I wondered what the hell was up with her when she started stripping out of her clothes. She wasn't cute in the face at all, but she did have a big ass and titties, so that was enough to get my soldier to salute for her. Once thing led to another and she was deep throating my dick like her name was super head. Since the head was on point, it was only right that I saw what the pussy was like. Shit, I had already cheated by getting my dick sucked, so I might as well go all out.

When Aniyah walked in and saw us, I was shitting bricks. I knew there was no way I could talk myself out of what happened. I never should have let Niyah leave upset like that. Instead of jumping in my car to chase after her, I stayed at the trap texting her while Shavon was riding my dick.

As soon as we were done, I started looking around for rings because that was the only way Aniyah would take me back. I loved her and didn't want to lose her, but I couldn't stop fucking Shavon. I didn't have feelings for her and I knew she was fucking other people. What we had was all about sex. I tossed her a few dollars here and there and she was good.

I got tired of tossing and turning, so I grabbed my phone and went out on the patio to smoke a blunt. I was halfway done when my phone started going off. I looked down at it and saw that it was Shavon.

I peeked through the sliding doors to make sure Aniyah was still sleeping before I answered.

"What do you want, Shavon?"

"Damn, that's how you answer the phone now?"

"Cut the shit, it's almost midnight. What do you want?"

"I'm outside your house, we need to talk."

"Are you out of your fucking mind?" I asked.

"Nigga, don't act like this the first time I been to your crib. I need to talk to you and you haven't answered all week, so I figured this would get your attention."

"Stay in the car, here I come," I told her.

I walked in the house and put on my sneakers and hoodie then headed down the stairs and out the door. I closed it quietly, careful not to wake Aniyah or the baby.

I opened Shavon's door and climbed in.

"Hey baby, did you miss me?" Shavon said with a smile.

"Wipe that fucking smile off your face. You know not to come here with Aniyah here."

"I know and I'm sorry. I just missed you."

"Drive up the block to the park before someone sees your car outside my house," I ordered as I let my seat all the way back so no one could see me. I didn't know my neighbors like that, but I couldn't take any chances.

Immediately after Shavon parked, she turned the car off and started digging in my basketball shorts trying to free my dick.

"What the fuck are you doing? You said you wanted to talk to me about something."

"I do, but first I want to take care of you. I know Niyah just had the baby so she ain't fucking you right now."

Shavon was right about that, so I laid back in my seat and let her do her thing. She was sucking my dick like her life depended on it. It was like she knew I was ready to call it quits so she had a point to prove. I was close to busting and she could tell, so she stopped and climbed over on top of my lap. She lifted the little ass dress she was wearing and sat on my dick. Her pussy clenched my shit, and I was trying my best not to bust until she at least got her one off. We fucked in the car for a good ten minutes before I pulled out and nutted on her stomach.

Shavon reached in the glove compartment and grabbed some wet wipes and handed one to me while she used the other ones to clean herself.

I felt guilty as hell fucking this girl again after the slick shit she pulled. Instead of me trying to make things right with my wife and cutting Shavon off, I'm still out here fucking around while she's lying in bed with my newborn child. It's crazy how I'm upset that Aniyah isn't a pro at sucking dick. I should be happy that my wife ain't been ran through. Instead of being patient and teaching her how to please me, I'm out here fucking a bitch who do dicks for money.

"I can't do this anymore, Shavon. We should have never crossed this line. After today, don't contact me anymore. The holidays are already awkward enough."

"Nigga, you got some nerves. We've been fucking over a year and now all of a sudden you got a conscience. Where was that conscience when you took me to get that abortion done because you didn't want your wife to know we were still fucking? Where was it when you fucked me on Thanksgiving night while your wife was in the other room?"

"I don't need you to remind me of all my fuckups. Everything I've ever done with you has been a mistake, and I'm sorry if I made you believe that we could be anything more than what we were."

Shavon held her head back and burst into laughter like she was at a comedy show. She was scaring the shit out of me because I didn't find anything funny with what was going on between us.

"Well, my nigga, the mistake you continuously made every chance you got created another child. I'm four months pregnant and it's yours."

I sat there dumbfounded because I couldn't believe I was this careless again. The only thing I could do now is convince Shavon to get rid of it.

NOTE FROM ANIYAH

What's up y'all it's your girl Aniyah coming through with a quick message. First I want to say thank you to y'all that's been riding with this series so far. You've read all about Kenzie's love triangle and the shit she's been through. Everybody's sooo in love with Kenzie but what about me? What about my struggles and relationship issues? Oh that's right, you've only saw a glimpse of my life.

I know you wonder why I act the way I do. Not to mention the bombshell that was dropped at the end of this books.

Well, that's where part 4 comes in at. I was going to have my own spin off regarding Quan's and I relationship but of course Kenzie won't let me be great. It's cool though because there's still more to her story. I know y'all didn't think Kenzie and Blaze's exs were just going to let them ride off into the sunset with each other without putting up a fight.

Stay tuned for part 4 to find out if Kenzie finally gets her happily ever after with Blaze or if he's not the man you all thought he was so she calls things off for good. You'll also find out how I deal with the Shavon and Quan situation. Will I be strong enough to leave my husband or will I forgive him and work on my marriage? All of your questions and more will be answered in the finale.

One more thing while I have your attention. Make sure to leave an honest review. The author loves to hear feed back from her readers. It helps her perfect her craft in upcoming releases.

Also, if you want to stay up to date with Sneak Peeks, upcoming releases, and contests join the mailing list by texting your email address to Keyword KevinaHopkins@22828. You can also keep in contact with the author via the accounts below.

Email: kevinahopkinspresents@gmail.com
Facebook: Author Kevina Hopkins
Instagram: @author_khopkins

ALSO BY KEVINA HOPKINS

Movin' Different 2: A Hood Millionaire Romance

Movin' Different: A Hood Millionaire Romance

A Chi-Town Millionaire Stole My Heart

A Chi-Town Millionaire Stole My Heart 2

A Chi-Town Millionaire Stole My Heart 3

King & Armani

King & Armani 2

King & Armani 3

I'm Just Doin' Me

I'm Just Doin' Me 2

Lil Mama A Ryder

Lil Mama A Ryder 2

When A Savage Loves A Woman

When A Savage Loves A Woman 2

The Autobiography Of A Capo's Wife

Every Dope Boy Got A Side Chick

Made in the USA
Las Vegas, NV
15 November 2023

80922423R00106